KNIFE FIGHT

Long Dog sprang forward and this time Slocum didn't spring away but threw up his arm so that both their knife arms locked in mid-air. At the same moment Slocum's free arm circled the Shoshone's neck, while Long Dog grabbed Slocum around the waist in a bear hug.

Locked together they went into a kind of dance as each tried to trip the other. Slocum suddenly kicked Long Dog's ankle and brought him to the ground. Locked together, neither let go his grip as they rolled in the grass.

Suddenly, Long Dog stabbed his thumb into Slocum's eye, and when the white man's hold slipped, he broke free. Then, rolling swiftly across the clearing he was up on his feet. Yet Slocum was equally fast and now stood facing him.

Suddenly, the Indian charged...

OTHER BOOKS BY JAKE LOGAN

OUTLAW BLOOD
MONTANA SHOWDOWN
SEE TEXAS AND DIE
IRON MUSTANG
SHOTGUNS FROM HELL
SLOCUM'S BLOOD
SLOCUM'S FIRE
SLOCUM'S REVENGE
SLOCUM'S HELL
SLOCUM'S GRAVE
DEAD MAN'S HAND
FIGHTING VENGEANCE
SLOCUM'S SLAUGHTER
ROUGHRIDER
SLOCUM'S RAGE
HELLFIRE
SLOCUM'S CODE
SLOCUM'S FLAG
SLOCUM'S RAID
SLOCUM'S RUN
BLAZING GUNS
SLOCUM'S GAMBLE
SLOCUM'S DEBT
SLOCUM AND THE MAD MAJOR
THE NECKTIE PARTY
THE CANYON BUNCH
SWAMP FOXES
LAW COMES TO COLD RAIN
SLOCUM'S DRIVE
JACKSON HOLE TROUBLE
SILVER CITY SHOOTOUT
SLOCUM AND THE LAW
APACHE SUNRISE
SLOCUM'S JUSTICE
NEBRASKA BURNOUT
SLOCUM AND THE CATTLE QUEEN
SLOCUM'S WOMEN
SLOCUM'S COMMAND
SLOCUM GETS EVEN
SLOCUM AND THE LOST DUTCHMAN MINE
HIGH COUNTRY HOLDUP
GUNS OF SOUTH PASS
SLOCUM AND THE HATCHET MEN
BANDIT GOLD
SOUTH OF THE BORDER
DALLAS MADAM
TEXAS SHOWDOWN
SLOCUM IN DEADWOOD
SLOCUM'S WINNING HAND
SLOCUM AND THE GUN RUNNERS
SLOCUM'S PRIDE
SLOCUM'S CRIME
THE NEVADA SWINDLE
SLOCUM'S GOOD DEED
SLOCUM'S STAMPEDE
GUNPLAY AT HOBBS' HOLE
THE JOURNEY OF DEATH
SLOCUM AND THE AVENGING GUN
SLOCUM RIDES ALONE
THE SUNSHINE BASIN WAR
VIGILANTE JUSTICE
JAILBREAK MOON
SIX-GUN BRIDE
MESCALERO DAWN
DENVER GOLD
SLOCUM AND THE BOZEMAN TRAIL
SLOCUM AND THE HORSE THIEVES
SLOCUM AND THE NOOSE OF HELL
CHEYENNE BLOODBATH
SLOCUM AND THE SILVER RANCH FIGHT
THE BLACKMAIL EXPRESS
SLOCUM AND THE LONG WAGON TRAIN
SLOCUM AND THE DEADLY FEUD
RAWHIDE JUSTICE
SLOCUM AND THE INDIAN GHOST
SEVEN GRAVES TO LAREDO
SLOCUM AND THE ARIZONA COWBOYS
SIXGUN CEMETERY
SLOCUM'S DEADLY GAME
HIGH, WIDE AND DEADLY
SLOCUM AND THE WILD STALLION CHASE
SLOCUM AND THE LAREDO SHOWDOWN
SLOCUM AND THE CLAIM JUMPERS
SLOCUM AND THE CHEROKEE MANHUNT
SIXGUNS AT SILVERADO
SLOCUM AND THE EL PASO BLOOD FEUD
SLOCUM AND THE BLOOD RAGE

JAKE LOGAN
SLOCUM AND THE CRACKER CREEK KILLERS

BERKLEY BOOKS, NEW YORK

SLOCUM AND THE CRACKER CREEK KILLERS

A Berkley Book/published by arrangement with
the author

PRINTING HISTORY
Berkley edition/February 1988

All rights reserved.
Copyright © 1988 by Jake Logan.
This book may not be reproduced in whole or in part,
by mimeograph or any other means, without permission.
For information address: The Berkley Publishing Group,
200 Madison Avenue, New York, N.Y. 10016

ISBN: 0-425-10635-7

A BERKLEY BOOK ® TM 757,375
Berkley Books are published by The Berkley Publishing Group,
200 Madison Avenue, New York, N.Y. 10016.
The name "BERKLEY" and the "B" logo
are trademarks belonging to Berkley Publishing Corporation.

PRINTED IN THE UNITED STATES OF AMERICA

10 9 8 7 6 5 4 3 2 1

1

The day had broken gently, the sunlight slipping over the land, winking on the cottonwood and crackwillow in the draws that ran through the surrounding prairie. The rolling country was greening. But it wouldn't be for long. Soon it would be summer. Soon the carpet of grass would turn to its familiar tawny brown.

Slocum had ridden over a swell of prairie and was now looking down at a wide, shallow draw through which wound a ribbon of water, lined with cottonwoods and box elders. It was in that moment of absolute stillness that his attention had been caught by rifle fire.

The man appeared to be alone in the face of the Indian attack, his grim situation revealing itself to Slocum the instant he rode through the thin stand of trees and saw some dozen braves closing in on him. He was down, his back leaning against a long flat rock, his legs outstretched in front of him, but with his rifle in his hands. Obviously he'd been wounded badly. Yet he was holding his own for the moment, aided by the cover of some more large rocks. Only it was clear too that he didn't have much time.

Slocum had reined his horse at the lip of the draw, and now quickly outlined his strategy. Surprise and speed were the elements he would count on, not to mention accuracy with the Sharps. All of this was running through his head as he dismounted, pulled the Sharps from its saddle scabbard, and positioned himself at the edge of the trees that looked down on the scene below.

It was just as he took up his position that the man's horse screamed and went down, shot through the leg. He lay there until Slocum finished him off as the Indians charged their quarry. Even before the attackers had time to register the sound of a new rifle—and the dreaded Sharps, at that—Slocum had swung his sights to the back of a running brave, elevated just a little, and blown his head off.

The second report of the gun was still echoing into the band of attackers as he changed position and fired again, this time also scoring. And again he changed position, shouting orders as though others were with him, and firing once more at the surprised and suddenly wary Indians.

The man under attack had started firing too, not afraid to use his remaining ammunition now that help was at hand. In a few moments the warriors had decided they'd had enough, and they vanished into the box elders and cottonwoods. Slocum could see that they were young, probably not seasoned braves, and he figured they were probably youths who had slipped away from the reservation for some excitement. And had found it.

Suddenly, as they vanished into the cover of the trees, Slocum spotted a head of yellow hair, a white face, and a pair of lithe legs kicking a spotted pony into a gallop. A captive? Probably. But he knew he hadn't much chance doing anything about it. They were on the run, and if he were to follow, they would simply lead him into an ambush, or even right into their camp, where there could be other unfriendlies. So probably they weren't off the reservation, as he'd thought, but could be renegades on their own, maybe even part of a larger band.

He didn't lose his caution. He waited. He waited a sound length of time before riding in to where the man was lying. And the first question that Slocum asked himself was what a soldier was doing alone this far from the nearest army outpost.

The man was about done for. His face was gray, his leg had been shattered by a bullet, and there was also an arrow sticking out of his thigh. He was in great pain, hardly able to speak, and what he did finally manage to say was all but incoherent. Beside him lay his empty cartridge belt, and two canteens, one with water, the other containing whiskey, which Slocum offered him. He kept holding his Henry repeating rifle, which was now empty. His uniform showed that he was in the mounted infantry. Slocum knew the closest detachment was at Fort Tyrone, no small distance away. He saw now that his shoulder was seeping blood from still another wound.

But the soldier was trying to speak, make sense, while he was swiftly dying. The words were jumbled—gold, money, a secret cache—studding his wild, uncontrolled conversation. There were names mentioned, but Slocum didn't recognize any, nor could he understand where this treasure or cache might be located. Yet, at the edge of death, the soldier's voice rose with insistence. Slocum could make no sense at all out of what he said, nor did the dying man answer any of his questions about his name and what he'd been doing here so far from any army outpost, and alone. He helped him again to water and whiskey, while the sun reached down to the tops of the mountains and the air began to chill. He knew there was no way he could get the man to town, to a doctor. He'd be dead before they traveled a hundred yards.

He looked over at the dead horse. A big bay gelding, the usual army remount. But what was the man doing out here? Looking down at him, Slocum found his thoughts lingering on the young woman on the spotted horse. She had to be white, for he'd never seen an Indian with corn-yellow hair. It occurred to him that she might simply be a legitimate member of the band, and not a captive. Not that it mattered. Not that he ever expected to see her again.

He looked again at the dead horse, and when his eyes returned to the soldier he saw that he was dead. He hadn't made a sound. Death had been as casual as the lengthening sunlight dropping onto the grass. And perhaps as kind. The sufferer was at least beyond his pain.

Quickly Slocum went through the dead man's pockets. There was nothing by way of identification other than a torn piece of paper with the word "Gandy" scribbled on it. A name? A town? Plus a few coins amounting to no more than a dollar. He checked the saddle bags on the dead horse. Only some clothing, army issue.

His horse started to spook when he lifted the dead man and slung him over the animal's withers. But he gentled the animal, talking to him in a sing-song voice and taking time. Then he tied the body to the saddle with pigging string, which he always carried, just like any handy cowpoke. It was going to be a long, slow ride to the town.

There was a lone star in the sky as he rode away. He

SLOCUM AND THE CRACKER CREEK KILLERS 5

was thinking how the soldier was more than likely a deserter. Perhaps the dead man had also been heading for Cracker Creek, as he had been, on his way to the Sweetwater. Well, no matter. He'd be going there now. It was the best Slocum could do for him. And the least he could do.

The proprietor of the Cut-And-Run Saloon and Dance Place, who happened also to be the postmaster, coroner, and justice of the peace of Cracker Creek, paused at his task of sorting the latest batch of U.S. mail that had arrived that morning. The sack of letters, newspapers, and magazines had been delivered for convenience to the Cut-And-Run. Judge Woolf Quimby believed in convenience, his own in particular. He was a big man with a big belly, and he stood in the middle of the barroom now, straddling the floor like a captain holding his ship in a high sea. He was also holding a magazine at arm's length in order to have a better view of its cover.

"By golly!" He breathed those boyish words in genuine wonder and awe.

In a jiffy he had taken a long knife from his baggy trouser pocket, tested the edge of the blade with his big calloused thumb, and in a couple of accurate strokes he had sliced the cover from the rest of the magazine. Again holding the picture at arm's length, he admired the lovely lady. It was indeed a very lovely lady, clad in low-bosomed silk and lace.

He crossed the room, took a pinch of flour from a barrel and mixed it with some water in a whiskey glass, then pasted the picture to the center of the mirror behind the long bar. He took a moment to look again at the fabulous creature on the cover of the magazine, then suddenly stepped forward, again swiftly drawing his knife. This time he slashed away the writing beneath the picture that identified the lovely as one Eva Ronbari, a famous actress with a world-wide reputation for both beauty and thespian accomplishment.

Yes, that was better; now he stood back and cocked his head. Only the picture was no longer Eva Ronbari, famous and loved by thousands; it was none other than Miss Dottie Finlightly, the love of Judge Woolf Quimby's life, who lived not more than a ten-minute walk from where the judge, postmaster, saloonkeeper, and also coroner, undertaker, merchant of Cracker Creek now stood in lovestruck adoration.

What luck! What luck to come upon such a likeness of his beloved and in such a surprising manner, in the mail sack! And how good it was going to be to see Dottie's reaction when he showed her this picture of "herself." The Judge smiled into his scraggly beard, wrinkled his long, thoughtful forehead, and then belched with soft satisfaction into the Cut-And-Run Saloon and Dance Place. His eyes swept the large room, ran up to the balcony above with its rooms for the girls, then back down to the swinging doors leading onto Main Street, and the doors leading to the dancing room and his private office. Yes indeed, the Cut-And-Run was surely the hub of his financial fiefdom.

At that hour of the morning the saloon was empty save for himself and Swede Pete, the old swamper, who lay in a snoring sprawl across three chairs at the farthest and darkest corner of the room. The Judge, who had spent three months many years ago in an Eastern college—he had forgotten the name of the place—frowned with distaste as he suddenly became aware of the snorer's presence in his moment of adoration. He spat vigorously at a nearby cuspidor, missing his target and hitting the side of the mahogany bar,

SLOCUM AND THE CRACKER CREEK KILLERS 7

yet not marking his inaccuracy, for his attention was suddenly taken by the swinging doors being pushed open and a big man entering.

The tall man was carrying a large and heavy burden over one shoulder. Quimby noted the big Colt at his waist, the ease with which the man carried his burden, and the clear, steady, penetrating look in his green eyes.

"I'm looking for Judge Quimby."

"You are talking to him, mister." He nodded at the body slung over Slocum's broad shoulder. "You got business for the coroner, I see."

"That is what somebody told me when I rode in."

Quimby nodded to an open space on the floor between two tables. "Better put him there," he said.

Slocum kneeled and dropped the body of the soldier onto the floor where his host had indicated, then rose, aware that the oldtimer in the far corner of the room had risen, almost strangling himself on a final snore, and now stood regarding Slocum and Judge Quimby with a peevish look cut deep in his face while he scratched his thin, bony buttocks.

"Pete, give us a hand here," the Judge said, the words rumbling out of his broad chest with judicial authority.

At that point half a dozen citizens who had witnessed the body's arrival on Slocum's horse arrived in expectant silence.

They were totally ignored by the Judge as he looked at Slocum and said, "Dead, huh." His glance at the corpse was casual; part justice of the peace, part coroner, and likely too, he must have been figuring undertaker costs.

"'Pears to be," was Slocum's laconic reply to this observation.

"Soldier boy."

"That is what his clothes say."

Woolf Quimby signaled one of the onlookers with a glance, a lanky young man not yet twenty with droopy eyes and a low-slung jaw. "Hendry, go through his pockets. See what and who. Might have to tell the army. Can't tell much what he looks like with all that blood on him." His big bronze eyes swung to Slocum. "Where'd you find him, or where'd you kill him—which?"

Slocum turned a hard glance on that question and on the place it had come from. And he felt right at his best as he said, "I will take a whiskey."

He watched the rueful look come into the big man's face, stopping at the corners of his eyes, however, the bronze eyes remaining as hard as knobs.

"It'll be two bits, mister," the Judge said, using the special tone he had for keeping customers in their place.

"I don't want your lightning rod," Slocum said.

"Trail whiskey's what we got."

"Keep it." Slocum turned on his heel and started toward the swinging doors.

"Hold it, mister. This is the law talking!" The voice had iron in it.

Slocum stopped in his tracks and turned evenly to face the Judge. "What law?" He could feel the anger rising in him and he wasn't about to hold it in, yet he wasn't going to be foolhardy either. But things had gone far enough with this big pompous ass, he figured. It was time for him to call the turn.

"I am the law in Cracker Creek."

"You appear to be about everything from cradle to grave."

The Judge sniffed at that. "An' sometimes I officiate in

a certain capacity even before the cradle, if you get what I am sayin'."

Slocum had to grin at that, but he was dead serious as he spoke. "Mister, I said I want a glass of whiskey. I didn't come in here to get arrested, married, buried, born, or get myself a two-bit shave and haircut. You got it?"

He heard the murmur running through the little crowd that had become larger even as he and Quimby were having their exchange.

"I see you're a man of few words," Judge Woolf Quimby said, and now there was good humor in his voice.

The crowd of onlookers accepted this. They were used to the Judge's changes of mood; sudden, unpredictable, moving from the volcanic to the sublime and back again in a wink.

"And I use them few damn seldom," Slocum said, completing the well-known utterance of Texas John Slaughter.

Judge Quimby had stepped swiftly behind the bar, with a laugh barking out of his open mouth. "It'll be Old Overholt," he said. He was beaming. "Like the cut of your rig, mister. Tell me where you found this feller." And his big russet orbs glanced at the body on the floor.

While Slocum drank his whiskey and told his story of the Indian attack, the Judge poured himself a drink and came around to the other side of the bar. They leaned against the bar, talking, their eyes on young Hendry, who was finding all the things Slocum had already come across —the coins, a knife, half a plug of tobacco, and a plain brass ring, looking like a wedding band.

"That it?" Quimby asked.

"Yessir, Judge."

"I got a notion he could be a deserter," Slocum said, as Woolf Quimby poured them both further refreshment.

"How come?"

"No papers, for one. Then, his Henry hadn't been taken good care of, nor his horse. This was for sure not a first-class soldier." As he spoke he was thinking of the slip of paper with the name Gandy on it that was now resting in his shirt pocket. For some reason he didn't bother to question; he simply didn't tell Quimby about it.

"You reckon the army'll be wanting him, then?"

"I'd say so." Slocum looked at the whiskey in his glass.

"Guess I'll wire the nearest outpost if I can figure where'n hell that would be," the Judge said. Then, turning, "Hendry, pack the corpse down to the icehouse. Get some men to help. He's likely to be staying with us a while till the army gets off its lazy ass and comes for him."

Hendry nodded. The boy's eyes seemed to be loose in their sockets as he regarded the Judge and Slocum. Slocum could see he was being careful, watching for which way things were going to jump.

Hendry and his two helpers hadn't been gone five minutes when the swinging doors slapped open and a man in a black frock coat and a clean plug hat with a bullet hole through it walked into the saloon.

"I will enjoy a glass of your best whiskey, mate," the stranger said, speaking to the imposing figure of Woolf Quimby, who had returned to the dry side of the bar.

As the Judge plonked the bottle on the bar and pushed forward a scarred tumbler in front of the dapper customer, he scowled. "Passing through, are you, mister?"

"That I am." The accent was strange, Slocum noted, and he listened carefully.

"But look here, I thought you Westerners were supposed to be taciturn, enigmatic, and in short, minded your own business."

The words were spoken with such sincerity, even innocence, that Slocum could barely repress the smile that rose in him. The stranger was either a dude, or putting on a really good act.

Quimby, on his part, was on the point of blustering, not knowing how to take such frank observing of Western custom.

Slocum saw that he was about to blast out with something or other, but he held his peace.

Meanwhile the stranger's roving gaze had found the picture pasted to the big mirror in back of the bar. His eyes widened, his mustache, which was slightly waxed, seemed to curl, his chest expanded. He was not a large man, but at that moment he appeared larger than he actually was.

"Crikey!" He breathed the unusual word, a slow, appreciative grin starting across his smooth cheeks. Slocum gauged him to be older than he seemed; still not sure but that he might be kidding the Judge, who, to be sure was no dummy. Maybe the stranger had more courage than good sense. At any rate, his open admiration for the picture on the mirror derailed any animosity that might have been building in the Judge."

"That there is a picture of a fine lady," the saloonkeeper, mayor, coroner, judge, and postmaster said, his voice lowering to a softer key.

Yet Slocum thought he detected menace in that voice, too. And he noted how the room had grown silent.

"Delightful!" The stranger stroked the corner of his mustache with his thumb and forefinger. "Positively a delight! A treasure, I'd say! Yes, I'd put it like that. A veritable treasure!" He coughed a brisk laugh into his fist, beaming at the hefty man behind the bar, and hunched his shoulders. Slocum noted how muscular they were. In fact, the man looked as though he might once have been a prizefighter.

Slocum again had the definite feeling that there was something false about him, as though he was playing a role. And the man's next words emphasized the suspicion.

Now his accent was different—to Slocum's fine ear, at any rate—as he dropped to a nasal, more American register and said, "I'd certainly go for a half hour with the wench!"

Slocum watched Woolf Quimby's jaw drop, and almost instantly clamp shut like a bear's. He snorted. Slocum caught the fury coming across the bar.

Quimby's right hand dropped down out of sight and came up in a blur of speed as, in a split second, the newcomer went flying back across the room, having been smashed alongside his head with a bungstarter.

The Judge had moved so fast that for a moment the saloon was paralyzed.

Slocum's hand had dropped to his gun, just in case. But he remained as he was, minding his own business, while the stranger crashed to the floor, knocking over two chairs as he went, plus an elderly sometime prospector named Snake River Elihu. Snake River rose shakily to his feet, grabbing at his crotch for support, swearing, glaring in unabashed contempt at Woolf Quimby, who stepped swiftly from behind the bar and stood glaring down at the man he had clobbered.

"I got a notion to take that there bungstarter of yourn and shove it up yer ass!" snarled Elihu, quivering with outraged dignity. He was half the size of the Judge and a good twenty years his senior.

"Shouldna bin in the way," the Judge snapped without taking his eyes off the downed stranger.

Woolf was still gripping that favored weapon of the server of spirits, the deadly bungstarter.

"Gentlemen," he intoned as the gathering remained standing in stunned silence, not to mention appreciation of their fellow citizen's awful prowess. "Gents, that feller lying there looks to be a corpse. Fact, as coroner my first look says it is so. And as the law in Cracker Creek I do hereby appoint you to be a coroner's jury. What is your verdict as to the cause of this here feller's likely death?" And he came around the bar and looked hard at the man on the floor. "As coroner, I pronounce him dead."

The judge seemed to hesitate, then fell to one knee—not in prayer, Slocum swiftly realized, but to conduct a more precise examination. This took less than half a minute.

"The man is dead." The coroner rose and turned to the group standing by. "Gents, your verdict as to the cause of death."

There was no hurry. Nobody answered immediately. All were staring wide-eyed, straining to maintain the composure such an occasion called for and which expediency demanded, as they regarded the Judge's heavy, dark jowls.

Finally, a thin man with a stringy neck and a dour, gray face under his black derby hat found his voice.

"Reckon it's a open-and-shut thing, Your Honor, sir. Man there obviously died of a heart attack. You all agree with that verdict, men?"

Everybody nodded, and one fellow allowed that the dead man undoubtedly died of fear at the very moment he saw the fearsome bungstarter appear from beneath the bar. "Died of fear 'fore he even got hit."

All concurred.

"Death through misadventure is how we'll put her

then," the saloonkeeper, justice, now coroner declared. "You men there, take the corpse down to the icehouse. And Cal—" turning to the thin man beneath the black derby—"Impound any valuables found on his person."

It was at this point that Slocum had a funny feeling and stepped in. "Anybody got a notion as to this man's name, identity?" he asked innocently.

"Indeed, that is the business of this court," Judge Quimby said firmly, working well into his role as the situation progressed. "That is the duty of the office of coroner. And Cal there will let us know in a minute if there is anything in the man's belongings leading to his identity."

Cal was about finished with his search of the corpse's pockets, finding a wallet, a small amount of money, a letter, and a brand new deck of cards. These items he placed carefully on the bar near Judge Quimby. "That's it, Judge."

"Not much," the Judge said. His thick fingers touched the edge of the little pile of money. "This'll go toward burial. And this here..." He picked up the letter and pulled out a sheet of paper. "Huh—huh... A drawing, it looks like. Can't say what it is. No writing on it."

"Can I take a look?" Slocum said.

The Judge's big head swung around. "Why? You know this feller?" And Slocum had his funny feeling again.

"Never saw him before in my life. But that looks like a map there. I might help you; used to be a government surveyor not too long ago." Slocum dealt the lie as smoothly as a fourth ace.

Quimby relented in the face of such ease and pushed the paper along the top of the bar.

Slocum could make nothing of the lines and dots. though it could indeed have been a map. But there was no writing on it, nothing even to show the directions of the compass. He pushed the paper back toward the Judge, who picked it up and folded it. "No help to us," he said, stuffing it back into the envelope.

By now two men, under Cal's direction, had lifted the dead man and started to carry him out of the saloon.

"Take him to the shed," Quimby directed, repeating himself, "and get him cleaned up for burial. I reckon we can get to it this afternoon." His head swung halfway around to the other men who had been watching. "Hendry, you get somebody, maybe young Burt Snell, and a couple of shovels. Find a place over by Tom Wilson. Be company for Tom; this feller looked to be a respectable sort, like maybe a drummer, even though he did have a dirty mouth. But this after. Right now, lay him in the ice house next the soldier boy, out of the way like." He picked up the deck of cards and laid them on the inside edge of the bar, obviously claiming them for the house. Then he picked up the letter and checked again to make sure there was nothing more in it than the paper with the lines and dots.

"What about his name and address?" Slocum said.

The Judge said nothing as he handed the envelope to Slocum. It was slightly torn, scuffed, and clearly had been knocked about. There was no writing on it. Slocum was about to hand it back to Quimby when he felt something with his thumb. The Judge had turned to one of the onlookers and swiftly Slocum lifted the envelope to the light to see it better. The little pinpricks were just barely visible. He dropped the envelope onto the bar as the Judge turned back to him.

"Think I'll play a little solitaire," he said, reaching for the new deck of cards that Quimby had put aside. "What do you charge for a deck?"

The Judge started to answer, then evidently changed his mind as a thought swept into his mind.

"Slocum," he said, musingly. "John Slocum, is it?"

Slocum nodded.

"I've heard of you." His eyes watched the crowd dispersing for a moment, then lowering his voice he said, "Got some business I'd like to talk over with you. You got some time?"

"Might."

The Judge threw out a sour chuckle at that, which was also half a grunt. "C'mon back to the office," he said. And over his shoulder, as he led the way, "You can keep the cards."

Slocum didn't say anything. He already had the deck of cards safely in his pocket, and he was thinking of the slip of paper he had taken from the dead soldier with the name Gandy scribbled on it. It had of necessity been a quick look he'd given the envelope which was now in Woolf Quimby's pocket, but he was certain the pinpricks had spelled the same name—Gandy.

2

Cracker Creek, on the border of the Indian Territory, had a present population of just under a thousand. People were leery of making a count. Not long ago Cracker Creek's mines had drawn thousands from all over the country, but when the mines had flooded the boom had bust and Cracker Creek became a ghost town, harboring gunmen on the run, gamblers laying low till something or other blew over, and a few diehards. But lately the settlers had come with their wagons, and they brought livestock. The town was rallying, thanks mostly to Woolf Quimby. Now the population was like that of a number of Western towns: transient, volatile, with a few solid, steady citizens who remained and hoped to—and indeed were—growing families to be rooted in the land. A small town, not overloaded with law, though appearences were kept by such as Clyde Hames, deputy marshal and former bounty hunter, and some other officials, most of whom resided in the pants pockets of Woolf Quimby.

The town was all wood. Some claimed it had been nailed together during a single drunken spree; others held that a fabled outlaw gang had shot the town's buildings together, using bullets for nails.

But the depot was plastered. Nobody knew why. In any case, the railroad spur that had been promised had failed to come through when the mines went bust, and so the depot had been put up for nothing. The building had gathered unwanted articles following the decline of the Golden Pig Mine: old parts of wagons, harness, broken shovels, axes in need of repair, and, for some unknown reason, a good many parts of beds, mostly the springs.

The sidewalks lining Main Street were eight feet wide and all wood except for the nails. There were no other sidewalks. The streets still grew grass, albeit with difficulty. An ordinance recently passed by the mayor and town council prohibited buffalo and other wild animals from running at large in the town's streets.

It was well past noon when Slocum stepped out of the Metropole Rooms into the glaring afternoon sunlight just as two young boys raced by, almost hitting him. Feeling refreshed from a bath, shave, and a square meal, he was in the act of lighting a cigar Judge Quimby had given him, but the near collision interrupted the action. He stood there on the wooden boardwalk, his eyes following the boys as they raced down the street. He struck another match against his thumbnail and lighted up.

Now, tossing the match away, he saw out of the corner of his eye a lady passing along the other side of the street. Without turning his head, he realized she was taking a moment to inspect him covertly. He looked over and smiled openly at her.

It pleased him to see the color rise in her smooth cheeks. She was decidedly his style, with large eyes in a wide face, and a figure that caused the blood to race in his loins. She had looked away shyly. Now he watched her as she walked carefully down the opposite boardwalk. For a moment he was tempted to follow her, but something caused him to wait. There was something strangely familiar about her.

Instead, he remained where he was, drawing pleasurably on his cigar, watching the girl who appeared to be enjoying the afternoon, a person really interested in her surroundings, it seemed. Like himself.

As he began strolling along the boardwalk, his thoughts returned to the conversation he had had with Woolf Quimby at the Cut-And-Run Saloon and he was struck—as he often was—by the coincidences that happened not infrequently in his life. The Judge had told him the harrowing story of the capture of his daughter by Indians. And suddenly before Slocum's eyes the big, flamboyant, bullying man turned into someone old, even soft, a man who had been scored by this terrible event. Woolf Quimby had been a good deal more than shaken as he told of the disappearance of his daughter Felicia and his futile efforts to find her.

"I would pay anything, Slocum—anything for her return."

"But what about the army? Didn't you go to the army?"

"Of course. Of course I went to the army!" Some of the big man's testiness returned under Slocum's prodding. "They tried. They sent out patrols. But they kept telling me it was probably a renegade band and they'd left the country. And by now—anyway, after three years..."

"Look, it seems to me kind of late in the game for the Shoshone or Crow to be capturing white women. We're supposed to be at peace."

"It happened. I went right away to Fort Tyrone and spoke to Captain Chiswell. A good man. He said he would send out a search party." Quimby spread his thick hands. "They have been looking, asking questions, ever since. But she's just disappeared!"

They had been seated at the round table in the back room of the Cut-And-Run, which Quimby frequently used as an office. He had ordered drinks sent in, and had offered Slocum a cigar. And money.

"Find her! That's all I ask."

"But are you sure it's the Shoshone? What proof do you have? I mean, was it even Indians?"

"They attacked the stage at Cripple Crossing. Felicia had been returning from her year in Boston, at school. I was expecting her any hour. Then news came the stage had been attacked by Indians. Everyone wiped out—except Felicia, who was the only woman on board. The whole outfit was wiped out, driver and guard killed and evidently tortured, and the passengers the same. The red devils! I tell you if I can get my hands on them...!"

Slocum held up his hand. The man was all but beside himself as his grief poured through him like boiling oil.

"Sorry, Quimby, but I've got to ask you—if you really want me to investigate; but if they did capture your daughter, and killed everybody else, then who was there left to tell the tale? How do you know for sure, for absolute fact, that the Shoshone got her?"

"There's no question! Dumb Dan Dorrance, an old prospector, spotted the band riding away from the area of the attack, and there was a white woman with them."

"But are you sure it was her?" Slocum insisted.

"If it wasn't, then where is she? Where is her . . . body?" At the last word his face clouded.

Slocum felt sorry for the man. Nevertheless, he pursued his line of thought. "But still, you've no proof. Look, I don't doubt your word, or the man who saw them riding off, but it is possible in such moments of excitement, shooting, killing and so on, to make a mistake."

"Maybe. But I'd bet my bottom dollar it is so."

"Are you keeping after the army?"

"What do you think?"

Slocum nodded.

"I've heard a lot about you, Slocum, and it's all the kind of stuff I want. I want you to find her, or at least find out what happened. Like I say, you can name your own figure. Believe me, I've tried everything: ex-lawmen, bounty hunters—I've written Pinkerton, Washington, the War Department . . ." He paused. "Slocum, if it would do any good I'd beg you."

Slocum had stood up then and remained for a moment looking down at Woolf Quimby, lord of the town of Cracker Creek, but a man humbled before the disaster he'd just related.

"Let me turn it over," Slocum said.

"I have heard you are good with the Indians, know how to handle them, and that."

"Nobody's good at handling the Indians," Slocum had said then. "But sometimes somebody can find a way to talk to them like they weren't somebody else's idiots."

"Gotcha."

Now, as he strolled down Main Street, the scene with

Quimby ran through his head once again. His thoughts too were on the white woman he had spotted riding with the band that had attacked the soldier and killed him. It could be just one more of those coincidences, but it was sure handy to think that Felicia Quimby and the girl riding with the braves who had wiped out the soldier were one and the same. It meant he knew where to begin. He hadn't seen Buffalo Horse since the trouble at Bullhead Crossing, and the Shoshone chief owed him a favor.

He was near the place where he had left his bag—the Metropole Rooms—so he turned in that direction. His hand, reaching into his pocket, encountered the deck of cards he had received from Woolf Quimby at his saloon. He'd forgotten the cards. Quimby's story about his daughter had driven the cards and the dead stranger in the bar clean out of his mind. But they took over now as he walked quickly toward the Metropole. He was remembering how Quimby had said that if it would do any good he'd beg. Well, why hadn't he begged, then? Why hadn't he?

He had told Quimby he would think it over, yet he knew he was more decided in favor of going ahead with the offer than not. Excitement drew him; it always did. Moreover, he remembered the fleeting moment when he'd spotted the girl riding with the Shoshone band and the thought flashed through his mind that he might indeed see her again. And he was curious too about Quimby, for he'd had that strange, strong feeling that Quimby had recognized the stranger whom he'd hit with the bungstarter.

He had reached the Metropole now and climbed the stairs to the upper landing and walked down the corridor to his room. He was thinking of the deck of cards in his pocket and the envelope with the pinpricks when he reached the door.

SLOCUM AND THE CRACKER CREEK KILLERS 23

Something made him stop. Yes, there had been that moment the room clerk had looked away when he'd walked in. And now the strangely familiar feeling sweeping through him. He knew that feeling like a fresh sense of himself, knew it best on the trail when there were fewer man-made distractions and the layout was more clear, more honest. On the trail a man had the elements and the animals to deal with, and only now and again men. But in a town there were always the twisted men, the men of greed and scheming. They congregated in the towns, figuring, he supposed, that in a town it was easier to hide. He had often thought of this, the restriction of a town, and the kinds of people, many of them decent men and women, but many the riffraff, the bullies, petty thieves, and killers.

And so he was all at once totally alert as he faced the door to his room. He knew somebody was inside. He knew it as he knew his own name.

Swiftly, and without any sound whatsoever, he turned and slipped down the long corridor to a window at the end. Lifting the sash, he leaned out and found that with his long reach he could climb to the roof which was directly above, the Metropole being a two-story structure. What was more, the roof was flat, so within minutes he was actually on top of the long building and had crept down to a place which he figured to be directly above his room. It took a few minutes, for he was careful to keep low and out of sight of anyone who might happen to look up from the street or from another building.

He was in luck. There was a fire escape, and a balcony just outside the room next to his. He judged the distance carefully, risking anyone chancing to look up and see him. But he heard no outcry; no one seemed to notice. It was getting to be evening and the pedestrians had their thoughts on dinner or diversion of some kind or other. His luck held and he felt like smiling when he saw that the window of his room, only a few feet away, was open. Somebody was pretty sure of himself; somebody was making himself right at home.

Who? He knew it couldn't be Woolf Quimby, yet he was the only person Slocum knew in town, and one who could be that brassy. But he had just left Quimby. Who, then?

He was waiting for a moment that would be appropriate to reach over, grab the sill of his bedroom window, and swing across and pull himself into the room. A crazy thing; he could get killed. On the other hand, he could get killed walking through his own door. Or he could just walk away. Then suddenly he smelled the cigar. The smoke was coming from his bedroom. Yet it wasn't the brand Quimby had offered him.

All at once someone released some firecrackers in the street below and a shout went up from several people. Looking down, he saw a horse bucking, almost unseating its rider, who was cursing a wild streak.

It was in the next moment he jumped, grabbed the sill with both hands, and pulled himself into the room. Almost quicker than taking his next breath he had drawn his gun and now stood slightly crouched, but with his attention at razor edge, facing the occupant of the room. Seated comfortably in the one chair the room afforded, the uninvited guest was quietly drawing on a pantella cigar, regarding him with amusement.

"Well, do drop in! I thought you'd never get here."

Slocum faced the intruder coolly. "I generally like to come home that way," he said. "Saves time and trouble if I have a visitor who isn't friendly."

"If I'd a gun I could have shot you."

"I didn't figure you would."

The surprise was genuine. "How come?"

"Not by the way you were enjoying that cigar. I could tell by the drift of the smoke. Pleasure and bushwhacking seldom go hand in hand."

"I'll have to remember that." The girl lifted the cigar to her mouth and took a slow drag. "I have to agree with that saying that a woman is only a woman, but a good cigar is a smoke," she said.

She had remained in the chair, still comfortably seated. Young, no more than in her middle twenties, he'd wager. And damn good-looking. For a moment he regarded her long black hair, which fell to her shoulders and then was tied up in a loose bun. She had widespaced gray eyes, a full mouth with full lips, and breasts that pushed provocatively at her cinnamon-colored taffeta blouse. But the main thing that impressed him was the expression in her eyes. The word was "fun," and there was a teasing in the way she spoke. She had a delightful nose, short, firm, and her eyebrows formed two perfect arches over eyes that actually reminded him of a cat he had once known.

"Would you like a smoke?" she said.

Right then Slocum decided that while he found her splendidly attractive he wasn't in the mood to spend any more time beating about the bush.

"Let's cut the how-de-do and get down to it. What do you want?"

He had spoken firmly, not too harsh, but hard enough so that she'd get off her dance. But she was really sure of herself; and he had to admit he liked it. "The question," she said, "is also what do *you* want, Mr. Slocum."

"I want you to take your clothes off and get onto that bed."

Her smile broadened. Reaching over, she laid her cigar in the stone ashtray on top of the washstand, and stood up.

"Consider it done," she said, and started to undress.

Seated at the big round table in the back room of the Cut-And-Run Saloon and Dance Place, the town council of Cracker Creek was in session. Judge Woolf Quimby was presiding over the five members, and had just filled them in on the "doings" in the barroom. With care, calculation, and even some charm, the Judge related in detail the recent events that had transpired.

The gathering listened, loyal out of necessity, it must be said, for Judge Quimby knew where an awful lot of bodies were buried. He knew how to manipulate, crush, and woo, and even in a number of cases talk someone into stupefaction, so that agreement was the only alternative to death through boredom.

And he loved anecdote. His tales could be interminable yet compelling. In short, he could charm, he was witty, and where money was involved—and where was it not?—he could be generous, especially when work was well done.

"We are presently addressing ourselves to the question of the Golden Pig," the Judge was saying.

"You have the latest reports, Woolf?" a man named Pat Terwilliger asked. "I for one have been waiting anxiously to hear whether or not we're back in the mining business."

A smile swept across the Judge's face. It somehow made him look younger. The table relaxed. Somebody coughed. Someone lighted a cigar. Terwilliger drummed his fingers lightly and not at all impatiently on the wooden tabletop.

"I think we can safely say that we are in business," Woolf Quimby said with a smile. The smile broadened in satisfaction. "Of course, let's not count our eggs too soon, but..." He held up a very thick forefinger. "But I've received word that we can pump the water out of Number Three Shaft. I've located the necessary equipment, and at a good price."

"That's better than we thought," a tall man seated next to Terwilliger said. He looked younger than the others. His name was George Allison and he owned the dry-goods store. This was one of the few enterprises Woolf Quimby did *not* own. He didn't even have an interest in it.

"Of course this is not to be known, not even whispered. Otherwise every Tom, Dick, and Harry will be storming in with old claims, messing up the whole affair." The Judge's words were spoken with his accustomed authority, which as a rule proved right and sensible.

"Number Three Shaft," said a short man with very black hair slicked down all around his bony head. He wore spectacles, and indeed looked like what he was, a banker. The manager of the Cracker Creek Bank & Trust repeated those words, "Number Three Shaft of the Golden Pig will shortly be in operating order. May we take this statement to be true?" Tod Allnutt grinned around the table, amid the nods and murmurings of his colleagues.

Pat Terwilliger turned now to the gloomy-looking man at his left, Herman Ronigan, barber and land agent. "Herm, I think this is going to be the turning point for Cracker Creek. We're really coming back."

All nodded at that; all were still steeped in the memories of the great bust that had taken place seven years before when the fabulous Golden Pig was flooded. Now, thanks to the heroic efforts of the five of them, led by Woolf Quimby, they were on the comeback trail.

The final or fifth man sitting at the table—not including Quimby, who made it six—now started coughing from the cigar smoke flowing into his face from Herman Ronigan's stogie.

"For Christ's sake, Herman, do you have to smoke that piece of rope indoors?"

The remark provoked smiles on a number of faces, but a scowl from Herman, who didn't have to change his face expression very much, since he was already in a dull mood. He simply shrugged and looked toward the head of the meeting for some support. None was forthcoming.

Muttering, the sufferer, whose name was Matt Mathews, quickly turned his thoughts from the disagreeable encounter toward the Cut-And-Run's fabulous new girl, Loretta, whose company he had left only a couple of hours ago on the balcony above the saloon's main room.

Woolf Quimby sighed again with deep pleasure as he let his thoughts roam through some of the high points of the past few years, and especially the last six or seven months. He had certainly swung it. The deal was his. He was bursting with excitement inside, wanting to tell someone, to strut and sing a brag on how he had given new birth to the Golden Pig when everyone—*everybody!*— had said it was impossible, that Cracker Creek and the Golden Pig were finished. Not so! By God, it was not so! He, Woolf Quimby, had pulled it out!

"I propose a toast to Woolf Quimby!"

Pat Terwilliger was on his feet with his glass of brandy held high.

They stood, their glasses held high, and toasted their man.

Woolf, meanwhile, was barely able to contain his unbounded joy.

But now Herman Ronigan was speaking. "God bless you, Woolf!"

They all drank.

"Now all we've got to do is get the other shafts back and we'll be swimming in gold," somebody said.

"No chance of that, I'm afraid," Quimby answered warmly. "But, boys, we're going to be rich as the kings of old on just Number Three. No fooling! We're going to be running one of the top shafts in the West. Sure, we'd love to have the whole mine drained, but an operation like that would drain the Treasury of the United States. And we don't need it. We're in for a fast killing with Number Three."

"And it won't be just the Golden Pig we'll be making money on," Tod Allnutt pointed out. "We'll hit it all around. By God, it's going to be a boom town again!"

They had all drunk a good deal, Quimby told himself. But they had earned it. He had earned it. By God, he had his secret, too, and that was what made it so much better. The secret. No one knew or even suspected, not even Dottie. And surely none of these here at the table, toasting their good fortune and his health and now even more in his power than before.

"Higher!" She gasped the word—the command—in his ear as he drove into her. Reaching down, he brought her thighs up onto his shoulders and drove as high and deep as he could, causing her to squeal again in ecstasy, her arms clutching him, her bucking legs thrown toward opposite corners of the room.

Slocum was bathed in sweat. The girl was unbelievable, insatiable, and the most satisfying he'd had in a good while.

He was clutching her quivering, bouncing buttocks, one in each hand, as they rode faster and faster to their bursting, almost crying climax.

Gradually their bodies subsided, still embraced, both sweating.

"My God, Slocum, you're a man!" She kissed him, then they lay together, letting the room come back to their awareness. Both were on their backs, looking up at the cracked ceiling.

"What's your name?" Slocum asked.

"Tony."

His hand felt along her damp thigh. "I'm interested to know how come you were in my room."

"Just had a notion. I'm a girl who works fast. I see what I want and I go for it. I spotted you in the Cut-And-Run."

"Quimby send you?"

"No."

He turned toward her, watching the side of her face, the curve of her nose, her cheeks. His eyes dropped to her young, firm breasts pointing toward the ceiling, still red from his kissing, the nipples softer than they had been.

"You believe me, don't you?"

"Maybe. You know Quimby, I reckon."

"I work for him."

"On your back, you're saying."

"Sometimes. It's a living. Other times I do some of his paperwork. Thing is, I liked your looks right off, Mr. Slocum, sir." Once again she was seductive, her eyes feeling over his face, lingering on his lips, her hand moving up along the inside of his thigh.

Once again he was erect. Now her hand found the tip of his organ and began playing.

They slept. Later, in the dark, for it was then evening, he took her again.

As she was leaving he was still careful, not sure about Quimby.

Tony was sharp, "I don't blame you for being suspicious," she said. "Here I come out of nowhere, and since I work for Quimby you've every right to be suspicious of my motive. But it's just as I told you."

"I believe everything I hear," Slocum said. "With everybody. And at the same time I believe nothing." He was thinking as he spoke how she must have come from a well-to-do background. Her voice was cultured; she had manners that were definitely "Eastern." But at the same time she worked in Quimby's cribs. Well, he knew she was by no means the first high-class young girl to go that trail. He would keep his caution; that was the thing. You lived longer that way.

She was smiling at him. "I'd like to see you again, Mr. Slocum."

"Call me John, Pony."

"All right, John. But the name is Tony, not Pony."

"I like Pony," Slocum said.

Her laughter tinkled into the room. "So do I."

After she had left him he remembered the new deck of cards. When he'd dressed he sat down on the edge of his bed and opened the pack. The coal-oil light wasn't very bright, but it was strong enough to show him the pinpricks on the backs of the cards, as he had suspected. He felt a sudden urge to take a closer look at the body of the man Woolf Quimby had killed with the bungstarter.

Night had fallen and the main thoroughfare of Cracker Creek was dimly lighted. Yet the town was very much alive, coming to a new surge of energy as darkness took over. Towns were like that, Slocum realized as he walked along the wooden sidewalk. Abilene, Dodge, Fort Worth, they all flourished in the dark. The very atmosphere was different with the sun not watching.

Slocum found himself walking down toward the Cut-And-Run and decided then and there to stop by before going to see the corpse that had owned the deck of marked cards. It seemed clear that the man had been a gambler, and one of the looser variety. When Slocum had examined the deck he'd received from Quimby he'd soon discovered that whoever had marked the cards knew his business damn well. With this in mind, he thought he would see what he could pick up at the saloon. Gandy? Was that the man's name? It had been on the paper in the dying soldier's pocket and it had been pricked on the envelope carrying the map that was now residing with Woolf Quimby. The two dead men had to be connected, then. Well, he decided, the corpse—Gandy, or whatever his name was—could wait. The dead man wasn't going to run away. Meanwhile, he would see what the gossip was at the Cut-And-Run where Gandy, if that was he, had been killed. There just might be something. He still had that feeling that Woolf Quimby had known who the stranger was. And he could easily catch up with the corpse at a later time. Gandy—he would call him that—Gandy wasn't going anywhere.

3

At the Cut-And-Run the game was jackpot poker, requiring a pair of jacks or better to open. The dealer was a dark-complexioned man with a drooping black mustache and very fast fingers. Slocum watched him closely, but without being obvious about it, as he stood with the small group of onlookers.

He was standing behind a big Texan trail boss who had just brought a small herd up the trail from the Red River country en route to Montana. The drovers had run into Indian trouble from a renegade band a day's ride south of Cracker Creek, and so the ramrod had decided to check the town for help. Two of his men had been wounded so he'd brought them into town to the sawbones, following the roundup of the stampeded herd. He had announced loudly in the barroom that he was looking for hands to finish the drive. The cattle were in a tight gather just outside the town and under a full guard. The man whipsawing the herd was clearly no one to argue, Slocum could see, and he was playing his cards carefully, sipping his drink and keeping a tight eye on his two cowhands. There were two drummers in the game to make it six, counting the dealer whose name was Delehanty. The big drover's name was known; Tex Leatherbee built a loose loop, it was said, along the trails running north and south. He knew how to use a running iron. Slocum wondered if the Indians who had raided the Texas herd might be the same band who had shot up the soldier, and had the white girl riding with them.

The room was crowded. Save for the faro bank, which wasn't open yet, the room offered just about every possibility a man could want for losing his money: poker of any kind, three-card monte, dice, chuck-a-luck, hazard, old sledge, the tobacco-box game, and there were two wheels of fortune on the walls.

Slocum was in no hurry to join the game, and when one of the drummers cashed in, offering his chair, he said no. Another man, who bought beef for the government and was traveling through on his way to Denver, accepted the empty place.

Slocum remained standing easily with the hangers-on. What he was really doing was listening for any bits of gossip that would be useful, at the same time that he was studying the players, and anyone else who came within his view.

Now his attention was suddenly drawn to a young woman whose arrival was creating a certain commotion. As she crossed the crowded room heads turned, men stepped back to allow her passage, and she was greeted respectfully on all sides. To Slocum's astonishment he saw it was the woman he had spotted in the street that afternoon, the one who had been studying him as he'd been in the act of lighting his cigar. Closer now he saw she was even better looking than he'd realized. Dressed in trim calico, with a high color in her cheeks, she nevertheless revealed an alarmingly provocative figure, though it was obvious she had dressed discreetly and with no intention of provoking comment or looks. Or had she? Slocum asked himself that question as he watched the swing of her buttocks walking across to the table near where he was standing. To his utter surprise he saw it was the faro table and that the woman was apparently in charge of it.

The room settled down now, but he kept his eyes on the brown-haired, brown-eyed young woman. She couldn't have been more than thirty, he decided. He watched her hands as she set up her game. They were small, very white, and well cared for, always a good sign. He felt the grin coming into his face and kept it back, not wanting to draw attention to himself. A woman faro dealer! Women gamblers were not common in the wild country, but there were some; however, he had never seen one with the looks Woolf Quimby's faro dealer carried.

Covertly, Slocum watched her set up her bank and make ready to play. He saw that she had an assistant with her now, a man, who would take care of paying and collecting the bets. She also had a casekeeper to manipulate the small box that contained a miniature layout with four buttons running along a steel rod opposite each card. It was the casekeeper's job to move the buttons along, as on a billiard counter, as the cards were played, so that the players could tell right away what cards remained to be dealt.

The young woman placed her layout with care, the suit of thirteen cards, all spades, painted on a large square of enameled oilcloth. The cards on the layout were arranged in two parallel rows, with the ace on the dealer's left and the odd card, the seven, on her extreme right. Ample space was allowed between the rows for the players to place their bets. In the row nearest the players were the king, queen, and jack, called the "big figure," and the ten, nine, and eight. In the row that was nearest the dealer were the ace, deuce, and trey, known as the "little figure," plus the four, five, and six. The six, seven, and eight were called the "pot." The king, queen, ace, and deuce were called the "grand square." The jack, three, four, and ten were the "jack square," and the nine, eight, six, and five were known as the "nine square."

The room was thicker now with customers, heavy with tobacco smoke and the smell of men as the young woman shuffled and cut the cards, then placed them face upward in the dealing box, the top of which was open.

Slocum knew that in the hands of an honest dealer, faro was considered the fairest banking game ever invented. In no other game was the percentage against the player so small. Indeed, with the first and last cards dead, the bank held no advantage whatsoever other than what might be found in the splits. And this was so slender as to make the game almost total chance.

During all her preparation she had kept her eyes on her task, hardly looking about the room after giving it an initial sweeping glance. But Slocum caught her looking at him, knew she'd recognized him as the man in the street; her eyes moved on without even a flicker of interest. He was delighted to see her again, and would have walked over to talk to her save for the fact that he had planned his visit to the Cut-And-Run for business.

He was still trying to sort out his impressions, trying to see which way he would go. He certainly planned to pursue his hunch regarding the gambler whom Woolf Quimby had killed, and the man's connection to the dead soldier. And maybe his connection to Quimby? Somehow he felt it was related to Quimby asking him to look for his daughter. Yet he couldn't have said how.

He had gotten the story pretty thoroughly from the Judge about the capturing of his Felicia, but it was always the in-between details that interested him when he was working on something. The little things that had been left out, a man's gesture or facial expression that came out unknown to himself and which sometimes gave away a point. Gossip was not reliable, but on occasion there would be something buried inside some juicy bit that even the speaker didn't realize.

The next time someone left the table Slocum sat down. There were five players besides himself, making six. The original spirit that had held the onlookers in the earlier part of the game had dampened. The two cowboys and their trail boss were still there, but the drummer and the man who bought beef for the government had dropped out, their seats being taken by a land speculator and a stringy, white-haired gentleman in an enormous black Stetson and flowing white locks whom everyone in the saloon seemed to know. To Slocum and the Texans he announced that he was the editor of the Cracker Creek *TaleTeller;* and reporter of the world's happenings. Slocum had heard of J. Orville DeWitt. He had a stentorian voice, nimble hands with thick veins and freckles showing, and deep-socketed, watery eyes under which ran dark gutters. Slocum noted that he smoked a top brand of cigar while addressing himself liberally to his whiskey.

The fast-fingered Delehanty served the cards skillfully. He wore a sparkling diamond on the little finger of his left hand. Slocum tossed in his cards on the first two pots, the two cowboys splitting as each won once.

On the third deal Slocum opened for the usual ten dollars on a pair of aces. He was sitting to the dealer's right. The dealer raised him twenty dollars. Slocum stayed and drew three cards.

Delehanty's pasty face lighted up slightly with a grin. He said, "I play these."

Slocum didn't help the aces. He had figured out what was coming, having studied Delehanty for some time. He knew what was coming but he didn't know how much he would bet. Delehanty threw a calculating glance at Slocum's chips, and then bet fifty dollars.

"I call," Slocum said, first pretending to hesitate, and then spread his hand face up on the table, showing the two aces.

Delehanty couldn't believe it. In disgust he threw his cards down. "Didn't you see I was standing pat?" he said, his voice thick with disgust. "How come you call a pat hand on a pair of aces?"

Slocum grinned wickedly. "It wasn't all that hard," he said.

Indeed, it was easy, for he'd known the dealer was bluffing. He hadn't been standing there studying him all that time without figuring his giveaway.

The deal had passed to J. Orville DeWitt. "It'll be straight draw," he announced in his deep, plangent voice. He picked up a new deck and removed the joker. He dealt swiftly, his veiny, freckled hands shining beneath the overhead lamp. Slocum noted how DeWitt's appraising eyes, sharp as two diamonds, had been studying him since he'd sat down. He realized again that the man who had announced himself as a newspaper editor and reporter of the world's happenings was a good deal more than simply that. The crow's-feet at the corners of his blue eyes told him that DeWitt was a man with a good sense of humor. He had, in fact, announced his profession as though challenging any and all to engage him in dispute. But Slocum also realized from the way the elderly man looked at him every now and again that he wanted to make contact; he must have heard of him, or perhaps he simply recognized a fellow "rebel." In any case, his curiosity had been aroused over the purpose, the meaning of J. Orville DeWitt.

DeWitt had started right off asking some of the players about the passage at arms between Quimby and his victim. He appeared totally unafraid of any sort of irritation on the Judge's part about his discussing the killing.

"I am simply trying to work out my headline for the next issue of the *TaleTeller*," he said. "As always, everyone will get a fair shake, but the *TaleTeller* stands on its policy of digging out corruption and evil always and everywhere, printing our stories boldly, and using good, simple English. That is to say, the English of our great country." His voice rumbled slightly over the last two words, like thunder or a roll of drums in accompaniment to the importance of such a statement. Nobody appeared to be listening, but this didn't bother the editor, publisher, reporter, and special editorial writer for Cracker Creek's sole organ of information and news, as was stated on the masthead. Orville DeWitt obviously lived in his own world, and as far as Slocum could tell he was enjoying it. Moreover, he played his cards with skill, amusement, and with a running patter of conversation, much of it anecdote, that bothered nobody and took the role rather like the music that now and again came from the adjoining room where the orchestra of

40   JAKE LOGAN

Billy Joe Canasta and his three co-workers were blowing, beating, and sawing at their instruments with great vigor.

On the first round with the new, loquacious dealer, Slocum passed. The next four players passed, making five in all. A sixth player, who had just joined the game, opened with a ten-dollar bet. J. Orville DeWitt came out with a twenty-dollar raise. Slocum called. Another man called.

Slocum drew one card.

"Gonna win it, eh?" Orville DeWitt said pleasantly.

The next man took three cards.

DeWitt said, "I play these," which meant he was standing pat.

The man who had called just before Slocum's play now checked after taking a quick look at his cards.

Without allowing time for even the bat of an eye, DeWitt bet fifty dollars. And Slocum was onto his game, knowing that the newspaperman must be figuring that he, Slocum, had backed in the pot and was drawing to a straight or flush.

When Orville DeWitt bet fifty dollars, Slocum raised him a hundred, with nothing to back it, but he knew DeWitt was bluffing.

Slocum was dead sure he was standing pat on a bust. The man who had checked didn't matter. Even if he had helped his hand he would think twice about calling, with Slocum having taken one card and raising.

The man who had checked showed his openers, two jacks, and folded.

Orville shook his long head sadly. "You lucky!" He threw in his hand. "Imagine drawing one card with all that money in the pot."

Slocum tossed his hand into the discards and quickly pulled in his winnings.

He was getting ready to deal, and had opened a brand new deck of cards. He was feeling the hard, sharp edge of the new cards in his hand when his attention was drawn to the Texas trailherder sitting opposite him. The big man, pretty drunk now, had his eyes directly on J. Orville De-Witt, but he included Slocum in his anger.

"You dealt seconds," he said.

DeWitt, who had started to rise, sat back down again.

"You and him is working together. All that fancy talk. You didn't fool Tex, not old Tex." His hands had been lying before him on the table, but now his right began to move back. "You fuckers!" he said softly, but with ultimate menace.

The group standing about the table was suddenly still. Nobody was moving. There wasn't even the sound of breathing. But Slocum, watching that angry cowboy's hand creeping toward the edge of the table, moved like lightning.

Without even a thought having time to pass through his head he had thrown the hard, new deck of cards right at the big Texan's nose. The crisp, minted cards with the sharp edges hit like a razor against the cattleman's nose and he let out a grunt of pain, momentarily blinded. His hand, sweeping toward his sixgun, was interrupted just long enough for Slocum to get out of his chair and shove the table into the other man, who had blood running down his face.

"Jesus!" he heard somebody saying. "Sharper than a goddamn blade, them cards!"

The Texan was on his feet, dabbing at his face to staunch the flow of blood. It wasn't a serious cut, Slocum could see, but it was undoubtedly painful. And the action had served its purpose. The angry cattle drover had been stopped.

But only momentarily. He now stood squared off against Slocum, the two men facing each other in the circle the crowd had swiftly provided.

"There is two of you buggers," the Texan growled. "I will whip your friend's ass after I take care of you!"

Slocum's eyes were also on the drover's two cowboys, who were flanking him, but just a little behind, their hands near their holstered guns.

"And *your* friends?" Slocum said.

"They'll stay out of it." He spat viciously on the floor. "Wondered what this town was like," he said, glaring around at the assemblage.

The room had become silent. Nobody moved, while all waited, ready to dive to the floor or seek some sort of protection should lead start flying. It seemed to be inevitable. Behind the bar, Woolf Quimby stood like a monument of impartiality. His hands were down, out of sight, and Slocum wondered if he was holding his bungstarter or maybe a scattergun.

"Anyhow," the Texan suddenly said, "my fight's with that son of a bitch." He nodded toward Delehanty, who had dealt earlier. "Maybe you was working with him—I think you was—but maybe you wasn't," he said to Slocum. "I got no real fight with you, stranger. It is him. Shit, he is famous for them fast fingers. He's been slickering us honest Texian boys this good while."

Slocum felt a touch of relief at the other man's backwatering, not that he had any doubts as to the man's courage, but it would have been a foolish waste for the Texan to take him on as well as Delehanty. He was also interested in Tex's use of the old word "Texian."

"I got no fight with you, Tex," the lean, swarthy Delehanty said. "And for sure I was not dealing seconds."

"I says you was!" The words were hard, even as dealt cards. There was no arguing them.

Still, Slocum felt a crease of doubt and suspicion when he caught the side of the Texan's face as he turned his head. The man was playing it too easy, backing off that way when it was he, not Delehanty, who had cut his face. He glanced quickly toward Quimby, motionless in back of the bar. Why had he let it go on? He surely had a shotgun back of the bar. And surely too he had men in the crowd who were there expressly for confrontations like this.

His question was soon answered. Suddenly the batwing doors swung open and a stocky, bandy-legged man walked in. He was wearing a sixgun low on his left hip, and a tin star on his dark hickory shirt.

"What's going on here?" he demanded, and there was no need with a voice like that for him to be wearing a star. He couldn't have been more than five foot five, but he was almost that wide, and with no extra flesh. Solid rock, with a jaw like a ledge; the words came out of him as though cut with a hammer and chisel. He had a very red face and looked like a man born angry.

"I said what's going on here, goddamnit?"

"An altercation at cards, Marshal Hames," J. Orville DeWitt offered. "The boys had a misunderstanding, but I believe the angry moment has passed." He beamed amiably on Marshal Clyde Hames, who did not beam back, but continued to scowl not only at Slocum and the Texan but apparently at the whole world.

"Get back to your gaming and whoring, then!" the marshal roared suddenly, turning on his heel. He stood stock-still again and surveyed the rest of the room. "Get back to the devil's work, damn ye!" He spat suddenly at the cold potbellied stove. Slocum noted how neatly dressed he was, almost like an Easterner, which he clearly wasn't. He wore a clean white shirt, a coat, and California pants tucked into his boots, which gave off a high polish.

"Our marshal is a man of parts," DeWitt said at his elbow. "Reads books, gets his pants pressed."

"Dry as a bone, though," Slocum said.

"He is a diamond," DeWitt said. "Not even Quimby and his gang can push him."

Meanwhile, the marshal had started out of the room.

DeWitt's breath was warm in Slocum's ear. "You might think a man like that to be a churchgoer—I am referring to his remarks on gambling and such—but you would be wrong. Marshal Clyde Hames is much too religious for such an activity. I do believe he tries to live like a Christian every day in the week, and not just for a few minutes on Sunday. On the other hand, I have no notion what that means."

"Good for him, then."

"Not so good for Cracker Creek," the editor replied jovially. "He is still Woolf Quimby's man, even while he remains his own."

The marshal of Cracker Creek was almost at the swinging doors when suddenly both batwings burst open and a long, bony man, thin as a whip, came pouring into the room. He was holding a big Navy Colt in his right hand, and all could see he was so full of whiskey he was almost spilling it as he charged right at Hames, roaring out obscenities about the injustice that the marshal and Woolf handed down in Cracker Creek.

"The law west of hell!" Seeing Hames, the big Colt swung up, but Hames was lightning, almost too quick to be seen. His own Colt was out of its holster so fast that later men said it was as though the gun butt had jumped up to meet the marshal's hand as it came down. The visitor hadn't a chance. All he could do was receive the stroke of the gun barrel across the side of his head and he was on the floor.

The marshal holstered his gun almost as quickly as he had drawn it, and looked down at the fallen man. "Violent fires soon burn out. Small showers last long, but sudden storms are short," he quoted suddenly, yet dully like a schoolboy, glaring at the crowd, which had come closer to him. "Bring him down to the jail so he can sleep it off," he ordered, to no one in particular. Then, in a quieter voice, "It is the Poet I quoted. The Bard. I cannot claim to have created such words!"

Following this extraordinary utterance he moved to the batwing doors, where he waited as two men bent to lift the man who had fallen from his own folly. The room remained for a moment in stunned silence until J. Orville DeWitt said quietly to Slocum, "He quotes. He quotes all the time. It's apparently his abiding love."

"Are they true quotes, or does he make them up?" Slocum asked.

"Fact is, I happen to be the only person in Cracker Creek who knows the stuff isn't his. That's one of the few times he gave credit to the author," he added.

"Was that really Shakespeare?" Slocum asked.

"I don't know," J. Orville DeWitt said. "But I can tell you Marshal Hames's great weakness. He blushes. It is uncontrollable. He has been seen to blush over things that are extremely slight. One would never expect it from such an apparent monument of strength, but he blushes like a ten-year-old schoolgirl."

The door to the second room burst open suddenly and the sound of music and dancing broke into the bar. The thud of feet, the "do-si-do" of the caller, and the fiddle, fife, drum, and cornet drove like a great pulse into the gaming room, bringing life back to where it had been before the tight little interruption which had been so neatly handled by Marshal Clyde Hames.

"Enough," J. Orville said softly to Slocum. "Enough evil for the day there of, if you won't mind my paraphrasing, sir!" He smiled benignly on John Slocum as the two men helped the pistol-whipped victim of Marshal Hames's rectitude to his feet and conveyed him out of the Cut-And-Run toward the town jail, where he could sleep it off—first, of course, having picked up the big Navy Colt and handing it to the marshal.

It was late when Slocum left the Cut-And-Run. Cracker Creek lay dark under the deep, starry sky. Slocum paused for a moment on the wide board sidewalk, inhaling the smell of horses and cattle and the big land. Somehow he felt that things were going as they should. He knew things always did, whether you liked it or not. Running into the unique Marshal Clyde Hames had raised his interest in the town. And furthermore, who was the faro lady? He had wanted to talk with her, but he noted that she had left by the time the action with the Texan took place. He'd missed his opportunity there. He decided he'd try the next night. He was in no hurry. Yes, he felt good.

He reached for a quirly. Too late he heard the movement behind him. The grip on his shoulder was like a vise as he was pulled around and the big knuckles landed on the side of his face.

The stink of booze and bad teeth told him instantly who

his attacker was. The next thing he knew a second blow crashed against his jaw and he almost went down. He regained his balance, sidestepping out of the way as Big Tex Leatherbee drove at him, his fists charging like hammers.

Again they faced each other and when Leatherbee swung, Slocum ducked, feinted, but suddenly slipped in some wet horse manure and went to one knee. Tex took the opportunity to drive his enormous boot into Slocum's ribs.

"Get up, you son of a bitch!" he demanded.

Slocum, still on one knee as the big man drove another kick at him, fell out of the way in the nick of time, only to be grabbed from behind by one of the cowboys, who tried pinning his arms to his sides while his companion slammed a fist into his stomach.

Instead of struggling Slocum suddenly let himself go limp in total relaxation. It served its purpose by throwing the two cowboys into surprise.

In the next moment he kicked Tex Leatherbee in the kneecap and then brought a sledgehammer blow of his fist against the doubled-up Tex's ear. The trail boss toppled like a tree to the ground.

But now one of the cowboys had tackled Slocum and he was also down, and getting madder every second. Pinned by the cowboy, who was gripping his knees so he could only move his upper body, he yet grabbed the second cowboy, who was moving in, and pulled him toward himself. Holding the cowboy's head in the crook of his arm, Slocum pushed his thumb into the man's eye. Screaming in pain, the cowhand released him. At the same time his companion loosened his grip on Slocum's legs. Slocum pulled himself free and tried to stand, but his legs were numb. He managed to roll clear and pulled himself up by grabbing the saddle rig on a horse standing at the hitching rail.

His vision was completely clear as he saw Big Tex Leatherbee charge right at him. He ducked and dove between the horse's legs. Tex was too slow to change course and crashed right into the animal's side. The horse, a big, tough buckskin, started to buck and kick, letting out a high whinny. Suddenly one of the cowboys let out a scream as a flying hoof caught him in the chest. He flew into the middle of Main Street and lay inert, either out cold or dead. Slocum didn't take time to wonder which.

Meanwhile the second cowboy had tried to tackle Slocum. Just in time Slocum brought his knee up under the man's chin, and it was two finished cowboys. That left a wheezing trail boss, who had regained his feet after crashing into the buckskin and now bore in on Slocum.

Slocum had it all together now. He jabbed two lefts into Tex's red face to straighten him up, then slammed a right into the pit of his stomach. When the big man doubled up he brought down a vicious right hook on the back of his neck. All three Texans lay face down in Cracker Creek's Main Street. As a newly arrived spectator put it, "Them Texans ain't going to go no place at all this good while."

The battle had brought a number of the clientele out of the Cut-And-Run, and the owner of the buckskin was among them, but by now the horse was no longer spooked. He stood snorting some, his lion-colored ears moving cautiously about.

"Got yourself a bit of extra help there, eh, Slocum!" It was J. Orville DeWitt with a huge wink and an elbow poked not too hard into Slocum's side. He was wearing a wide grin as he surveyed the defeated warriors in the street.

Slocum didn't answer him. He was looking over at

Woolf Quimby, who had just arrived on the scene and was looking down at the three Texans.

"Jesus," somebody muttered.

Woolf Quimby was not happy. He wasn't at all eager to reap the animosity of the Texans and the rest of their crew. He was not pleased with what Slocum had done. At the same time, he realized he had picked the right man to go after his daughter.

"You gents will excuse me," J. Orville DeWitt exclaimed suddenly, as though caught in astonishment. "I've got to get out my next issue. I think we've got another colorful story about the romance, allure, mystery, and excitement of our colorful, glorious western hamlet—the one and only and never-to-be-forgotten CRACKER CREEK!"

Chuckling wildly at his own ironic humor, he strode down the street, first stepping elaborately across one of the cowboys, who was just beginning to stir. "Read it in the *TaleTeller*," he called down to the fallen Texans.

4

Slocum was still thinking of the faro lady at the Cut-And-Run when, feeling slightly sore about the body, he walked into the Gem Eatery for breakfast. He had discovered the Gem's good Arbuckle coffee the day before, the sourdough biscuits, and the steaks. For him the atmosphere was congenial, especially this particular morning. It was in sharp contrast to places like the Cut-And-Run. For one, the Gem was quiet. Time to think.

He hadn't gone down to take a look at Gandy in the icehouse the night before, but he planned to do so as soon as he'd had his coffee and breakfast. At the same time, he was still thinking about Quimby's offer to hire him to look for his daughter. It would be an especially good notion right now, for he was sure the Texans would plan to retaliate for last night's doings, when he'd whipped the three. That humiliation would be hard to take, especially for Leatherbee.

It might be good for him to keep low for a while and try to find the girl. The Texans could be a nuisance. Trouble seemed always to follow him, no matter where he went. He gazed ruefully into his empty coffee cup. Well, all he had to do was ride on out. It was all he ever had to do, really. And it was what he never did. Why had he come to this place? Simple. He'd been on his way to the Sweetwater and had ridden into the Indian attack. Why hadn't he just ridden on? For him there was no place like the Sweetwater, and he tried every year or so to get back to that good country. He needed that now. He had needed it before riding into Cracker Creek, before finding the soldier. Why hadn't he just ridden on? Hell, he reflected, he might never find the answer to that one.

He ordered another cup of coffee. It was good sitting there in the Gem with the early morning sun on the window. Only one customer besides himself at the moment, an oldtimer down at the end of the counter slumped into his steak and sourdough biscuits. Slocum sat at the table by the window and looked out into the morning street. And suddenly he saw her.

She was walking slowly, but obviously with the intention of getting someplace, and in a moment she would be abreast of where he was sitting. Was she coming to the Gem? Then suddenly he knew why she was familiar, especially why she'd seemed so familiar last night at her faro bank. He remembered the man he called "Gandy" looking at the picture pasted onto the big mirror behind the bar in the Cut-And-Run. It was her, or at any rate a damn good likeness. Slocum felt his heart race. She was almost at the Gem.

Without another thought he stood up, paid for his breakfast, and stepped out into the street, almost colliding with her. It was a good opening, for it gave him the opportunity to apologize.

"I see I have really bumped into you," he said with a broad smile.

She said nothing. Her face was neutral, neither friendly nor hostile, as she nodded and moved to pass by him.

"Would you join me for a cup of coffee, Miss? My name is John Slocum."

"Thank you, no." She looked directly at him for a second only; then her eyes moved away, beyond, toward wherever it was she was heading for.

She was gone. He stood there watching after her in the nearly deserted street in the early morning. Where was she going? Where had she come from? She surely didn't look like any of the women gamblers he had seen or known. She looked much more like a schoolmarm. Did she work during the day, perhaps in a store? Slocum was intrigued, not only because of her beauty but her style. Her cool, open manner challenged nobody, yet accepted the fact of whatever was going on. There was something fresh, very clean in this. Well, by golly, he had only begun. If she wanted to turn him away from her, she was going about it in a very wrong way. And he was grinning to himself as he saw the leader of Cracker Creek coming toward him.

"Well, Judge, are you up early, or up late? You look in poor spirits." Slocum immediately spotted the sour note in Woolf Quimby and so had instantly decided to flush him.

"A public servant's work is never done," Quimby said in a ringing tone. Then his glum face gave way to an expression that was rueful. "You had mentioned, Slocum, I believe to someone—yes, Hames—that you hoped to take a look at the body, our friend the Englishman or whatever he was, who ran into the Cut-And-Run's bungstarter."

54   JAKE LOGAN

"I did." Slocum had indeed spoken to Hames when he'd run into him in the street after the battle with the three Texans.

"I'm afraid you're too late," Quimby said. And his eyes were partly closed as he looked at Slocum.

"What do you mean, late?"

"I mean the body is not there."

"Somebody took the body?"

Quimby, his broad hands sunk into his deep pockets, sniffed, spat, surveyed the street for possible listeners to their conversation. "No. Neither Clyde Hames nor myself feel that anybody *took* the body."

"Then what? It—he walked away?"

"That is precisely what it looks like, Slocum. There was no sign of anybody being in the icehouse. Not a trace. I checked it all over with Hames."

"I want to take a look."

"That is why I've come for you. Your rooming house said you'd gone out for coffee."

They had started walking and were within sight of the icehouse.

"What about the soldier?" Slocum asked.

"Still there. And it seems you were right. He was a deserter. Clyde got a reply from Fort Tyrone."

"What was his name?"

Quimby blinked. "The company records have him down as Private Nat Kovis. But there is a suspicion, a strong one Hames told me, that Private Kovis is not the real name. The real name was apparently Charlie Wills." He paused, cocking his head sideways at Slocum. "That name mean anything to you?"

"Not at the moment."

"Charlie Wills was a member of the Clay Gandy gang

that used to work around Sunshine Butte, not far from here, a good while ago."

Quimby had stopped just outside the icehouse, and now faced Slocum. He seemed to hesitate. A moment passed while Slocum turned it over. Yes, it made sense; Wills, obviously a road-agent sort, had been hiding out in the army and had been on his way to meet Gandy when the Shoshone had caught up with him. It made good sense.

"Have you decided about Felicia? About my daughter?" Quimby's question interrupted Slocum's line of thought. "I'll try to find her. I'll want to talk to you more. Get some information about her that might help me. Her habits, her attitudes about certain things."

"What the hell good will that do?"

"Quimby, when you're trying to do something with the Indians in this country here, it doesn't hurt to know everything."

"I'll tell you what I can," Quimby said, suddenly a good deal less belligerent. "Do you still want to check the icehouse?"

"I do."

"You know, I got a notion he was a card mechanic. That deck of cards. Who carries a brand-new deck around like that? He looked like a slicker to me from the moment he walked in."

But in the icehouse Slocum found nothing that would help him know what had happened to Gandy. It was simply obvious that he hadn't been dead, and had come to at some point and pulled himself together and walked away.

"You were pretty sure he was dead," Slocum said after examining the icehouse for any signs.

"So was everybody else."

"Let's go, then. This place isn't exactly warm."

It was a log cabin almost filled with big blocks of ice that had been cut from the river and were now packed in sawdust. In some places the ice was stacked to the ceiling, plenty of it, to serve the drinking habits of the town's inhabitants as well as passing strangers. There was also a cleared area where bodies were kept when necessary. The soldier lay there now, wrapped in a blanket. He was completely covered, and some big blocks of ice had been moved around him in an effort to preserve the body longer.

"Army coming for him?" Slocum asked as they went outside.

"They're pretty sure who he is, but they're sending someone to check his identity anyway. If he's a deserter he'll likely be buried here. I'll have to see what their man says."

The sun was hot on them as they left the icehouse and started down the street.

"Slocum."

Slocum turned his head to look at the man walking beside him.

"Slocum, you'll find my daughter, won't you?"

J. Orville DeWitt was in form, declaiming as usual from high authority. "It has been said—and not even I can improve upon it—that it is only a question of whether the editors of our present glorious era in the Great West die of whiskey or from gunpowder." He was leaning back in his easy chair, looking down his long nose at John Slocum, who sat facing him on the wooden chair with no back.

J. Orville now reached for his glass of whiskey, which was within easy grasp, and drank. Wiping his mouth vigorously with the back of his hand, he surveyed his visitor with a gleam in his china-blue eyes.

SLOCUM AND THE CRACKER CREEK KILLERS 57

"And I heartily concur with the notion that the powder, generally being of better quality, will likely accomplish its end first." A throaty chuckle pulsed up through his long neck and bounced into the room, bringing to Slocum the odor of booze and tobacco, and so reminding him of big Tex Leatherbee.

"I guess I've come to the right place, then," Slocum said amiably. "You are obviously the gent who knows where the bodies are stashed."

"And you want me to help you."

"I spotted you as a man of high intelligence right off," Slocum said with a wide grin.

This bantering exchange was taking place in the office of the Cracker Creek *TaleTeller*. It was a tight room, that is to say, bulging with a printing press, a big rolltop desk which was stuffed beyond capacity with papers, books, a few bottles, pens and pencils, a towel, ledgers, old newspapers and magazines, some envelopes, part of a sandwich, and a can of peaches, to name only the more evident articles. There was a torn rug lying on the uneven wooden floor, from which loose threads and holes offered a hazard to the unwary, two upended crates offering themselves as wooden chairs for visitors, a torn Union flag on the wall, slightly lopsided, and some flyers on wanted individuals, but severely outdated, to the point where they could soon be considered antiques, a jumbo stove, and a coal scuttle. The two windows were grimy and almost impossible to see out of. On the other hand, nobody could easily see within, which the proprietor, J. Orville DeWitt, regarded as the other side of the coin. In fact, J. Orville was a man who invariably took a look at "the other side of the coin" in argument, in indecision, in the most simple things of everyday life. It was something to do with his philosophy of life, his way, which was on the optimistic side, and very definitely unrealistic. He was, after all—he told himself— a creative person. An artist of the pen and print, devoted to the news. Frequently he avowed a devotion to the Great Calling, railing against the cheap newshawkers in the cities and the dishonest scriveners expounding on the West. He had also a remarkable memory, which was already proving useful to John Slocum, who had been inquiring about Cracker Creek, about Woolf Quimby, and about the name "Gandy."

"Gandy, you say?" J. Orville's lips pursed in thought, his brows lifted, pushing a web of wrinkles toward his snow-white hairline. "Gandy dancer—what they call those fellers working along the track, I believe." Leaning his sharp old elbows on the arms of his ancient chair, he made an arch of his fingers and touched them to his lips. He swept on. "I would know. I've been in this country, man and boy, going on this good many decades. But wait!" Suddenly he sat upright in his chair, his back as rigid as a drill sergeant's. "I just was idly musing and said 'gandy dancer.' You know, there was a man named Gandy, an outlaw. But no, no; I'm letting my imagination run away with me."

"Go on," Slocum said, leaning forward with his forearms on his knees. "Keep talking like that. Maybe we could find something."

The newspaperman reached for his glass, chuckling with appreciation at Slocum's enthusiasm. "Just so long as I get a story for the *TaleTeller*." He paused briefly to drink.

"Clay Gandy is the feller I'm thinking of. Ran the outlaws like a business for a good while, back when the mines were open. Then he got shot up, the law got him, and he was sent to, I believe, Folsom." He started rummaging in his desk while he continued to talk.

"Tell me about the mines," Slocum said, remembering how the soldier's incoherent talk as he was dying was spotted with reference to mines, gold, and loot.

"Well, you likely know about this place being a ghost town—until recently, at any rate."

"I know the mining was big in Cracker Crack and up on the Gulch."

"Real big. I mean, you could mention it in the same breath with the biggest in Nevada and California. The Comstock didn't shade Cracker Creek by much."

"Then I heard they ran out," Slocum said, reaching into his pocket for a quirly.

J. Orville swiftly passed him a Havana. "Water. Water did it. The mines flooded overnight. The town was wiped out. A tragedy. I mean, people were ruined. It was tragic!"

Slocum remembered hearing about it. Cracker Creek had been famous for its gold, which assayed in top figures. And then one day—disaster, and the town was emptied.

"It was Woolf Quimby pulled things together," DeWitt said. "I don't know why. He had his reasons." He chuckled. "Woolf always has his reasons. Anyway, he got things moving. Got people to come in and run cattle. Got a couple of herds up from Texas and almost had a railhead here, but the Union Pacific balked at the last minute. Politics! But I hear now they're going to pump the water out of Number Three Shaft." He sniffed, blew his nose between his fingers into the coal scuttle, then whipped out a brilliant red bandanna and wiped vigorously. Pocketing the huge bandanna he stroked his mustache with his long, bony fingers, his light blue eyes gleaming with self-satisfaction.

"But the press in those days, Slocum—my paper—we were on wheels!"

"How come?" Slocum asked. "You mean you ran your press in a wagon?"

"Myself and my partner, Cal Frontenac, we printed the *TaleTeller* all over the West, moving from settlement to settlement. Sir, I want you to know that Cal and I introduced the art of printing to most of the West. We issued our paper from four states and territories as we rolled across the continent. When we hit Cracker Creek, the big mining strike was in full swing. Within two weeks over five hundred buildings shot up. You get that? More than five hundred! So we moved our printing office from the wagon to this here." His hands swept in an arc to include the premises.

"You were here at just the right moment," Slocum said, though there was no need for him to say anything.

"You're wondering what happened to Cal Frontenac, but you're too Western to ask outright."

Slocum grinned.

"Cal got the croup and he up and died. He's planted over there at the town cemetery." His long thumb jerked over his shoulder to indicate the direction of the cemetery and the present residence of his former partner.

"So you're going it alone now."

"Had to. My friend, being a newspaper editor in this country, and by country I mean the West, is tougher than being a town marshal. I have been shot at, ordered out of town, and run out, too, threatened with lynching, tar-and-feathers, not to mention lead poisoning. It's a miracle Cal died in bed. I do not expect to. One story I printed here brought a vigilante bunch down on me; they were about to stretch me to the nearest cottonwood and throw my press into the river. But Quimby and Clyde Hames saved the day. And my friend here," he added, patting the holstered gun at his right hip.

"You survived," Slocum said. "You don't seem to have that kind of trouble now."

"Now things are different. The boom, of course, turned out to be a colossal bust. Cracker Creek settlement emptied as fast as it had filled. A few stayed. Quimby, Hames, yours truly, and a few others."

"Are you pretty close to Quimby and Hames?" Slocum asked.

"Not at all. They hate my guts, but they respect me. And in a strange way, I respect them—Quimby because he's such a devout windbag, and Hames because I hope to live long enough to see him laugh or at least smile. The man was born with a lemon up his ass. We live under an armed truce. Though I must admit..." He chuckled richly as memory took him. "I must admit I've come close to trying those boys' patience. You see, it's the old saying, Slocum; with us newspapermen, it's like—I forget the feller's name, but he was and still is one of the real old-timers in the craft—anyway, he put it that we want a story every morning that will justify someone waking us up before noon with a gun and the promise of death." He chuckled appreciatively at his words and then said, "You get my point."

"Tell me about this fellow Gandy," Slocum said. "He was here when you arrived?"

"Before. But he had the reputation. Clay Gandy. Used to ride with the Youngers, and more than likely the James brothers as well. Then he built his own enterprise." Suddenly he sat bolt upright. "By God, that's how I got 'Dancer' into it—hell, I am senile, like you are thinkin',

Slocum. The Gandy Dancer gang. That's what the paper played up. That name. It's coming back to me now! Gandy had a partner named Dancer. I'd heard he double-crossed him. Of course, Gandy was a son of a bitch."

"And you say he's in Folsom?"

"That's where he was. He did escape, but they caught him and took him back. He could have gotten out again, for the matter of that."

"How old would he be?"

"Not old. Forty or so, I'd guess."

"Have you ever heard anything about a cache of money; maybe from some bank hauls or stagecoach holdups. A big cache."

"My friend, I have heard endless stories of Clay Gandy's big hauls and how he cached a great wealth someplace near here. Thousands, the stories go."

"What if Gandy escaped from prison and was on his way back here to pick up such a cache?"

"All I can say to that is I hope you'll read about it in the *TaleTeller*." J.Orville chuckled hugely. "I am serious," Slocum said.

"You're suggesting Gandy and the feller with the funny accent could be one and the same," Orville said, serious now as he took in what Slocum had proposed.

"The feller Quimby hit with his bungstarter."

"The poor dude who had the stupidity to ogle Quimby's amour!" He sniffed. "Could be. That accent, the funny way of speaking you mentioned; I seem to recollect hearing Clay Gandy was Australian."

"I say maybe." Slocum took a slow drag on his cigar. He was looking thoughtfully at his companion. "By the way, what is this business with Quimby and the famous Eva Ronbari? I heard a rumor that he wanted to change the name of Cracker Creek to Ronbari. I've heard he's got pictures of the lady all over the place, that he writes to her constantly. The man sounds a bit loco."

"His organ of pleasure, my friend, may be loco—as whose isn't?—but let me assure you that Woolf Quimby is anything but loco. That man has the gall, the brains, and the drive of a small army. If he had fought with the South, Lee would never have surrendered. Be careful! Be very careful with that man, Slocum!"

"And so this explains why neither his wife nor his fourteen children object to his passion for the beautiful Eva."

"Indeed, that does explain it. But you have laid eyes on the equally gorgeous Dottie, have you not?" J. Orville was staring at him with huge amusement.

"I do believe so," Slocum said ruefully. "And she is quite a gal, I'd say. Question: What does she see in Quimby?"

"That is my question, Slocum, my friend. I suspect it's everybody's."

Unaccountably, the editor of the *Taleteller* fell silent. A fly buzzed against one of the grimy windowpanes, through which extremely weak sunlight entered the room.

"But Quimby has a weakness," Slocum insisted. "All strong men do."

J. Orville sniffed. "You mean like Clyde Hames?"

Slocum nodded.

"It isn't Ronbari and it isn't Dottie. They—or she, as the case may be—fill his passion, or consume it in possibly an imaginative way," Orville added. "But Woolf does have a weakness. Slocum, you are a perceptive man, and I appreciate that."

"His daughter."

"His daughter, Felicia," Orville repeated softly. "He

will move earth and heaven to get her back. She was taken by the Shoshone."

"He's asked me to find her."

"That won't be easy, Slocum, though maybe for you it won't be so difficult. But I understand it's not Buffalo Horse's band of Shoshone that has her, but some renegades. The army hasn't been able to find out anything."

Slocum thought of the Indians who had attacked the soldier and the white girl on the spotted pony, but said nothing to DeWitt, who had relighted his cigar and poured another drink for both of them.

After another short silence Slocum said, "Did you ever see his daughter?"

"She was a lovely young thing, taken when pretty young. Maybe like three, four years back. Woolf was tireless with the army, with gunmen, with anybody he could get his hands on. Like yourself. Knowing you, your reputation, I could have predicted he'd brace you. Tell me, you going to give it a try?"

Slocum looked at the end of his cigar, which he held in one hand. He seemed to be studying the ash.

"I might give it a try," he said.

"There'll be money in it for you. Woolf is generous."

Slocum lifted his eyebrows a little as he looked thoughtfully at J. Orville DeWitt from under the brim of his Stetson.

"What are you thinking?" DeWitt said, his eyes sharp on Slocum.

Slocum took out a wooden lucifer and struck it along his pants leg. He held the light in one hand, the cigar in the other. He was looking straight at Orville as he said, "I am still wondering just why he clobbered that feller with the bungstarter. That hard, I am saying. I mean, he like to have killed him. Fact, he thought he did."

"You don't think it was on account of what he said about Eva, do you?"

"I am not sure." Slocum dropped the match to the floor and put his foot on it, then lifted the cigar and took a drag. "One thing, when he told me that the body had gotten up and apparently walked off, he was pretty shook. Course, it ain't usual for a feller you figure to be a corpse getting up and walking off. But I've had a feeling this good while that Quimby knew him, or maybe just knew *about* him, knew who he really was. There was something going on there more than the scenery. I think there are more than a few people concerned with the cache Gandy is supposed to have hidden. By God, if it's as big as the rumors say, I'd be concerned myself."

The frame had opened with Dottie the faro dealer covering a couple of large bets, losing one and winning the other. After she had passed the dice to Slocum, she watched closely while he came out on a five and offered to borrow on the four-three draw for five dollars.

"I'll make it for ten dollars," Slocum said.

"Make it twenty," the girl said, shoving in a stack of cartwheels.

Slocum called almost simultaneously with the throw of the dice.

The girl's soft white hand flashed under the overhead lamp as, without even looking down, she reached out and caught the dice. "Ten more you don't make it," she said as she threw the dice back to Slocum.

Slocum counted out the money and threw the dice hard

against the table railing. They spun around for a moment before settling.

His face was expressionless as he kept his eyes on the girl. And it seemed the entire dice game and all the onlookers froze at that moment.

"Aren't you going to look at your throw?" Her voice did not carry the lilt which he had found so attractive when they'd talked together outside the Gem Eatery. Now it had an extra something in it—a challenge.

"I know what it is," Slocum said. He had still not looked down at the dice lying on the green baize, but he had seen the two spots of color come into her cheeks.

"Something the matter here?" The voice of Woolf Quimby boomed into the dramatic scene, and the onlookers stepped back, giving the table and the participants in the drama plenty of room.

"Nothing as far as I'm concerned," Slocum said, and he kept his eyes on the girl as Quimby came up behind her.

"You think something is wrong with the dice, mister?" the girl asked, her voice cutting across the table. In the next moment there was nothing in the room but silence.

"No," Slocum said easily, and the expression on his face said nothing more than that. But all noticed how close his hand was to his sixgun. "Man can't beat the four-three, that's for sure."

"He didn't even look," somebody said to Quimby, who was staring hard at Slocum.

Quimby had it by now and a smile swept into his face. He turned to the girl then. "Dottie, my dear, I guess you haven't met John Slocum. He is a new arrival in town. I should have told you. Mr. Slocum might be here a while with us. And he should receive our every courtesy."

She kept her eyes on Slocum, a cold smile coming to

the corners of their mouths as she said, "Thank you for letting me know, Judge. Mr. Slocum and I have already met, but I had no idea of the sharpness of his perception—and wit." Her smile broadened suddenly. "Mr. Slocum, I apologize for this misunderstanding, but you were given a straight throw." As she spoke, she reached forward and picked up the dice and tossed them to him. He had to admit the switch she pulled right then was grade-A.

"I don't doubt you for a minute," Slocum said in his most courteous voice, feeling the straight dice again in his palm. "And I would like to have another throw."

"I'd like to let the pot stay."

Slocum nodded.

"I'm Dottie," the girl said.

"I know," Slocum said.

Quimby was smiling as the game resumed.

5

"You really surprised me there, Slocum. I mean, claiming I switched dice on you."

"I wasn't *claiming* anything. You *were* switching tops and flats. And I let you know it. Now let's change the subject."

She had been waiting for him as he'd left the Cut-And-Run, asking if they could talk, so he'd taken her to the Pastime, almost directly opposite his rooming house.

They'd found a table in a corner which, even though the room was crowded, offered a certain privacy. He was intrigued by the change in her. The time on the street when he had asked her to have coffee she'd been as prim as a schoolmarm. Later, seeing the way she dealt faro, and especially how she handled the dice revealed a completely different Dottie Finlightly. He wasn't sure yet which one he preferred, but he wanted to find out.

"You came pretty close to making yourself a tough enemy there," she said now.

"Quimby."

She inclined her head, then raised it to look directly at him. "Woolf Quimby sort of thinks I am his," she said.

"You, or Eva Ronbari?" Slocum asked carefully.

She gave a little laugh. "All those pictures! But it's understandable."

"How do you mean?"

She hesitated, then said, "I don't mean to be nasty, but have you seen his wife? She is not the most beautiful woman in the world, nor the youngest."

"And you are."

"Is that a question or a statement, Mr. Slocum?"

"Take it any way you like," he said with a grin, his eyes moving down from her lips to her full bosom.

"You might not like the way I take it," she said.

"I think I can decide that."

"Do you think I'm dreadfully bold?" she asked.

"Refreshing," he said. "But you're so obvious; still it's obvious to me that you want to be obvious."

"You think Woolf sent me."

"I do. Just as you wanted me to spot you switching tops and flats."

Her laughter was genuine. He was admiring the softness of the skin on her face, her neck, her small but capable hands.

"Well, suppose that was so. Why would I do that? Why would I intentionally be obvious, and why would Quimby sic me onto you?"

Slocum thought he had the answer to that. He was pretty sure Quimby was covering something that he didn't want discovered and was risking it in the search for his daughter. But he said nothing, remembering again the false note in the Judge's voice when he'd almost begged Slocum to help him. Only he hadn't begged.

"You have a lovely earlobe there," Slocum said, his eyes on the edge of her left ear as it peeked from beneath her soft brown hair.

"You decline to continue the subject, sir?" she said with a tinkle of laughter.

"Not at all. I am continuing our original relationship," Slocum insisted.

"From when . . . ?"

"On the boardwalk outside the Gem."

She looked down at her hand, which was holding her glass on the table. "I should tell you that Woolf is a very jealous person. Very jealous."

"I never thought he was not," Slocum replied. "After all, why shouldn't he be?" And he looked directly into her eyes.

She looked down. "It's getting late."

"Tease over?" he asked as they both stood up.

"What do you mean?" He saw he had touched her as her cheeks flushed and there was a flashing in her eyes.

"You know what I mean."

"I suppose I do," she said, returning immediately to her former self.

As they walked outside into the street he accidentally brushed her arm, and she withdrew elaborately. For an instant he felt anger mounting in him, but curiosity supplanted it. He wanted to know what was going to happen next, and he didn't want to cut anything off.

"Would you like to walk me to the door, Mr. Slocum?"

"Sure. I'll even walk you *through* your door," he said with a grin.

"That will not be necessary."

And it wasn't, he soon found out. She didn't live far away from where they'd had their drink, and when they reached her building, which he supposed to be a rooming house—or perhaps her family's, for there were lights showing in two of the windows—she turned and bid him good night.

"Have you ever read an author named Rudyard Kipling?" Slocum asked.

"Yes, I have." She turned away abruptly toward the door of her house.

"Then perhaps you're familiar with his verse that goes, 'The Colonel's lady and Mollie O'Grady are sisters under the skin.' Good night." And he touched the brim of his hat and left her.

Slocum walked up the street toward the Metropole in a state of puzzlement. The girl's strange behavior alternated between an open, even inviting attitude on the one hand, and on the other a hard refusal, so marked that he found it extraordinary. He wondered just what she was to Woolf Quimby. Not to mention the question of why she had bothered with him at all, why she had cheated at the dice game. Had Quimby put her up to it? If so, why?

As he progressed along the street he found his irritation rising and decided he didn't feel like sleeping right then. So he stopped in at a saloon called the Easy Chance and had a whiskey. By the time he'd finished one drink he felt sleepy and started back to his room at the Metropole. His thoughts were still on the girl. She was alarmingly beautiful, and he wondered if maybe that was the problem. Maybe it was all too easy for her, with the men flocking around. Maybe she got her kicks out of such games. Maybe it was as simple as that. By the time he reached his

SLOCUM AND THE CRACKER CREEK KILLERS 73

rooming house he'd decided he'd had enough of Dottie Finlightly, at least for a while.

Once again he had that feeling he knew so well. It came as he mounted the stairs and walked down the corridor to his room. But this time he didn't hear anyone inside the room, and there was certainly no smell of cigar smoke.

She was lying on the bed and sat up immediately as he struck a match to light the coal-oil lamp.

"How did you get in?" he asked.

"Same way you did." She held up a room key.

"You make your own or did you steal it?" he said after he'd turned up the wick.

"Woolf Quimby owns the Metropole Rooms," she said.

She had brought a bottle of champagne and two glasses.

"May I do the honors?" Slocum said, his eyes moving pleasurably over her full bust which was straining at her ruffled gown.

She sat on the edge of the bed and he took the one chair the room offered, and faced her.

Expertly, Slocum opened the bottle, the cork hitting the ceiling as it was released with a loud pop.

He had been standing as he opened the champagne, realizing that her eyes were all but actually feeling him. He thought the cloth of his California trousers would rip.

"What shall we drink to, Mr. Slocum?"

Slocum filled her glass. "To champagne, of course. Listen to that beautiful fizz."

He put the bottle down, lifted his glass high, his eyes on the girl, who was totally different again, the opposite of the schoolmarmish, rigidly correct, and judging "lady."

As if reading his mind, she said, "Why not drink to Mollie O'Grady?"

"You said it!"

Her whole body seemed to be smiling as she raised her glass. Her eyes were dancing on him and he felt his passion surge.

"Do you have any sisters?" he asked.

"No. Why do you ask?"

"Just didn't think there could be anybody else that good-looking," he said. "Unless you had a twin." The thought of her having a twin had sprung into his mind as a result of thinking about her changing behavior.

"Sorry. No sister, no twin. I am kind of mercurial, I guess. I've been told that I am. And I can see it, too."

"Mercurial?"

"I change a lot."

"I know what the word means," Slocum said. Then he added, with a lowdown, sowbelly accent and tone, "Hain't so goldang sure on how to put the spellin', howsomever."

They both chuckled at his imitation of an old sourdough fighting the language.

"This time let's drink to passion," Dottie said.

"I'm all for that."

When they had drunk the toast he leaned forward and took her hand, moving his chair closer to the bed. "See, when I touch this part, just at the base of your fingers, and your palm... He moved his fingers lightly over the palm of her small hand. "That stirs something in the rest of you, doesn't it?"

"Hmm..."

"Would you agree?" he insisted playfully.

"Oh yes, surely yes." She slipped her hand on top of his. "Suppose I take your thumb, say, or this middle finger ... and hold it. I could stroke it like that. Wouldn't that give you a feeling of something moving inside you?"

Slocum could feel his erection straining like a club at his trousers as she began slowly to stroke his middle finger in her fist.

He started to speak, but she bent down and put his finger in her mouth. The next thing he knew she had reached across with her other hand and was squeezing the head of his organ through his arched trousers.

"Does that give you a feeling?" she asked in a soft tone, and she began to unbutton his trousers with her free hand.

His organ was so hard she had to use both hands to get it out of his trousers.

"I can't wait," she whispered, tickling it with her finger right under its head. Her laugh was delightfully wicked as she stood up.

Slocum could bear it no longer and suddenly brought her down to sit on the edge of the bed. He began undressing her as well as himself.

The bed was wide, and noisy, but neither of them cared about that. They would have had it on a rockpile, Slocum knew. She sank back now, totally naked at last, as he feasted his eyes on her firm, high, quivering breasts with their big pink nipples. Her legs spread wide, but he didn't mount her yet. Instead he kneeled and rubbed the head of his organ in her belly button.

"That's good, good—good. My God, it's good," she gasped, hardly able to get the words out. "But this will be even better," she went on as she moved down underneath him, lifting her head so she could take him in her mouth.

Slocum thought he would explode. At last, almost at his peak—and she was expert in knowing just where he was—she released him, gasping for air. Then she grabbed him like a club and he plunged into her.

Slocum rode her high, tight, and fast, holding her bucking buttocks, probing deeper and deeper until he found just the place he was searching.

"My God... oh my Heaven! Heaven!" she cried softly into his ear.

Slocum was blind, weak, yet strong as a wild bull, riding her until a muffled scream broke from her into his neck and then he thought he was going to smother with his face buried in her quivering breasts.

Then, taking a nipple in his mouth, he sucked and chewed until she begged for mercy, and so he worked on the other one. In their fantastic passion he almost slipped out of her, she was so wet. And finally she begged, cried at him, pleaded, "Please, oh come, come, please come."

Without a sound the day broke over the mountain peaks, washed down into the valleys and box canyons, the sunlight growing stronger as it tinted the leaves on the cottonwoods and box elders lining the wide, swiftly moving river. The banks of the river were barely holding the water as it swept along, gray in color from the snows that had melted in the mountains. Here and there, chunks of ice that had broken away from somewhere along the way floated along, carrying branches, small limbs, and general debris from the thaw.

John Slocum rode to the top of the cutbank and drew rein. With slow, exquisite care his eyes moved over the countryside. The little spotted pony beneath him twitched his shoulder at a deer fly and shook his head, his mane flying, his bridle jangling. The great plain stretched before the man and horse like an enormous brown blanket, the grass dry and brittle from lack of rain.

"Dry enough you can hear it," Slocum said to the horse.

And it was so, as they continued to sit there in the still, knitting silence of the enormous day.

He had slipped out of town early, picking up his horse from the hostler while it was still dark, riding out while the town slept. And just as he'd left the dust of the huddled collection of log houses and frame buildings a cock crowed, then a dog barked. And then he lifted his horse to a brisk canter, leaving Cracker Creek and its interesting inhabitants behind him.

Now, sitting the horse as he surveyed the wide country with the river cutting down the long, wide valley, he thought of what he was going to do. He thought of how impossible it was going to be. Felicia had been gone for three years, and neither Quimby nor anyone else had any certain information as to who had captured her, or even if she was still alive.

He had just skirted a low butte when he saw the little figures in the distance. They were in single file, moving slowly up the side of a long, wide draw. They would have spotted him, he knew. But he had deliberately taken that chance, for he needed to get a long view of the terrain ahead, and he wanted the Shoshone to know he was in the country and he was looking for the girl. By the Shoshone, he meant Buffalo Horse and his braves, not the band of renegades which had killed Charlie Wills, the deserter, and which he'd heard were in the country and had been raising hell amongst the settlers. He had had occasion to deal with Buffalo Horse some years back, and he trusted him. It was his hope that the chief might give an angle on how to locate the girl, so he could get her back. He hoped Buffalo Horse remembered him. He had to start somewhere. Buffalo Horse owed him something, and if he could get Felicia without a lot of people getting hurt—including maybe the girl—then so much the better.

The bluebirds danced through the yellow flowers; they were everywhere. In the long draws and tall timber the mule deer, the elk and pronghorn antelope moved gently. There were still a few buffalo. In the Indian horse herd, spotted colts tried their skinny legs, falling down and getting up to run and fall again. In the mountain air the tinkle of the grazing bells was like a song. Many of the old people said it was a good sign, yet speaking carefully, hedging against false hope. For in general the times were hard. Again the agent man had failed them, blaming the long delay of rations and supplies on the father in Washington when everyone knew he was hand in hand with the gray men, the outlaws who killed and stole even from their own people. There was sorrow in Buffalo Horse's tribe. Even so, the spirit lifted on such a day as this. For there was beauty everywhere, as far as the eye or heart could reach.

The Shoshone had been at peace with the whites since the big fight on the Wooden River, as the whites called it, and now they were camped only two sleeps away from the town called Cracker Creek and longer from the soldiers. The young men still burned for revenge against the soldiers, but Buffalo Horse and the elders of the council had insisted that they curb their anger. And for a while it had been so. Buffalo Horse's people had been making no fighting, only going out for meat because there was almost nothing coming from the agency, and the winter had been a long one, and cold. Still, there had been no fighting.

However, there had been the taking of the white girl by Long Dog and three other young ones more than three winters ago. Long Dog had been spoken to by Buffalo

Horse and the elders, and was ordered to return the white girl, for word had come that the pony soldiers were coming and the whole of the people would be punished for what Long Dog and his three friends had done. The soldier leader had come with his men and Buffalo Horse had spoken with them, but by then Long Dog and the three had run away, taking the girl with them. And then, because the soldier camp was far away, nothing had followed save for a message sent from the leader of the soldiers' camp saying again that the girl must be returned. But Long Dog and his followers were nowhere to be found. They had left the country.

Recently word had come to the camp that Long Dog had returned to the country south of the Wooden River where the Shoshone were camped and had even raided one of the stage wagons and frightened some of the white settlers. And now the news had come that a pony soldier had been killed, and the thought was that Long Dog and his band had done it.

Still, with the moon growing again, the land awakening to the longer days and nights, the people were ready to hunt. The older ones were hoping too that a big hunt would ease the restlessness of the young warriors.

The day had broken softly over the camp. The sunlight slipping over the tipis had paused on the cottonwoods and crackwillow in the draws that ran through the surrounding prairie. Much of the rolling land was greening, but this wouldn't be for long. The sea of grass would soon turn to its familiar brown. And next year, the old ones predicted, there would be less buffalo, less game to fill the parfleches.

In the lodge of Buffalo Horse four headmen sat with their chief in council. The men had entered the lodge with full care and respect, paying attention to all the necessary details which the occasion and person of their leader required. They had seated themselves in the required order, and they had smoked, letting the pipe move around the circle in the required manner.

"It is good," Buffalo Horse said.

"Heya," the others said in reply.

"What of the news brought about Long Dog?" asked one of the headmen. His name was Owl and he was the youngest of the group. He often spoke out against the whites and the injustice they had done to the red man.

A murmur of concern ran through the circle of older warriors now. News had been brought of Long Dog's return to the high country, with more warriors who had run away from other bands. Long Dog's band had been seen not more than a day's ride away, and yes, the Wasichu woman was said to be still with them. It was in the valley running down to the Wooden River where Sees Quickly and Birdsinger had been visiting relatives.

"The soldiers will surely come again to ask about the Wasichu woman," a headman named Tall Walker said. "The captain man said so last time. And it is near the time. He said the soldiers would come again when the grass was this high." He indicated with his hand held over the ground near where he was sitting. "They will ask again where the white woman is."

"Let them go find," Owl said harshly. "Let them find Long Dog and fight with him." Owl's eyes flashed. Then he paused, feeling Buffalo Horse's eyes on him.

"One needs to remember how to speak in council," the chief said.

"Grandfather, forgive me," Owl said, and turned to Tall

Walker. "I was in anger against the whites, not against any who taught me so many things, and still does teach me."

Tall Walker remained silent.

"There is the soldier man killed by Long Dog and his warriors," Buffalo Horse now said gravely. "I do not know if the other soldier men know this, but soon it will be told them, and they will be even more angry."

The headmen nodded and murmured in agreement.

A long silence fell, broken only by the guttering of the pipe as each smoked and pondered.

"What can be done?" a headman named Flying Fox said.

Now Buffalo Horse spoke. "It is so," he said. "We know we cannot fight the Wasichus, for we will have nothing." He looked at Owl, who had stirred. "We will have even less than we have now. And there are the women, the children." He waited a moment, and his voice was deeper when he continued. "The Wasichus are more than the blades of grass. They do not fight as the Shoshone fight. The whites rub out everything and everyone. They destroy. What is important is that our people live. If we fight there will be none of us left either for the dead or the living. There will be nothing."

"What can be done?" Flying Fox asked again.

A long silence fell into the lodge.

Finally, Buffalo Horse spoke. "We will wait. We will send men to find Long Dog and invite him to come to council."

"We have tried that," one of the elders said.

"We will try again," Buffalo Horse said. "There is nothing else we can do."

When they had left the lodge, the Shoshone chief cleaned his pipe and filled it. Then, offering it, he prayed.

All that night Buffalo Horse sat in his blanket. When one of his wives brought food he refused it. There was so much to trouble the heart. He would go to a high place and build a smoke lodge and purify himself with the heat from the sacred fire. And he would cry for a vision, and maybe then he could dream. For he must find the good road for the people. He could not act truly only from himself. Never could it be that way. For he was weak and could not see. The true road for the people could only appear from the Above.

When he saw the morning star in the sky he rose, wrapping his blanket around him. His body was as firm as the flight of the eagle as he walked away from the Indian camp.

6

"I want to know what the hell is the matter with you, letting him get away like that!"

Deputy Marshal Clyde Hames stood still as a stone while Judge Quimby stormed up and down his office at the Cut-And-Run like a conestoga wagon on a rampage. "Made me look like a complete fool! I'd pronounced him dead, for Christ's sake! And he just ups and walks away."

"So why did you pronounce him dead?" Hames asked.

"Because he *was* dead, God damn it! Least, he seemed dead. Looked dead, felt dead, wasn't breathing, didn't move a twitch. Anybody survive the way I hit him had to be made of iron, is all I got to say."

"Well, he is gone."

"I know, fer Christ's sake! Now, where the hell is he?"

Clyde Hames spread his shiny hands apart, palms upward, shrugging. "I got no idea."

"That's a big help."

"You sure it was him, are you?"

"I know it was him. Why'n hell you think I hit him so hard? Bastard could've upset our whole game here, and now more'n likely he will, unless...!" He drove his thick forefinger toward Hames's staunch figure. The marshal seemed to be growing right out of the floor, he was that stolid. Nor did he take a step backward under Quimby's threatening finger, eye, and general unleashed wrath. "Unless *you* find him, Hames!" Quimby concluded his outburst with a scarlet face, flaming eyes, and even with a touch of foam on his quivering lips.

Clyde Hames still stood his ground. He had been described in the *TaleTeller* not very long ago as "phlegmatic" in the face of danger. J. Orville DeWitt had chosen the precise word. Hames was as "phlegmatic as an empty stone jug."

But Woolf Quimby knew how to get him to ringing. "Hames, you know that I know—"

"Got'cha," the marshal said. "No need to draw us a whole picture book of what you know, Judge. I got'cha."

"Then you get'cha ass onto your pony pronto and find that son of a bitch Gandy! And I mean right now!"

Hames had survived Indian attack, a gun duel with the likes of Clay Allison, a couple of cattle stampedes, plus numerous Texans trying to tree the town, and other confrontations in the Great West. But he still revealed his reactions in the face of Woolf Quimby's threat by blushing. Even in the midst of his fury the Judge was impressed by this strange habit of the tough marshal—the tough gunman who helped him maintain the law this side of hell, as he and some newspapers were fond of proclaiming.

"Woolf, I will do as you say. We are in this together, remember?"

But he didn't like it, and he knew Quimby knew he didn't like it. He had always cursed himself for his great weakness, his red face whenever there was an untoward incident taking place. Ever since he was a small boy there had been that terrible problem—through childhood, school, and young manhood, and now at the age of forty he still couldn't control himself. In fact, the more he tried the worse it got. Even now, thinking of it, he found himself reddening even more deeply.

Quimby had calmed down enough to breathe evenly. "Right, Clyde."

The use of his first name told Hames that things were smooth again. He wasn't afraid of Quimby, but at the same time he tried to avoid the man's temper. Quimby, after all, knew too much about him, just as he did about Quimby. It was a useful situation, Hames realized, and for that matter so did Woolf Quimby. Each depended on the other.

The trouble was the sudden and totally unexpected appearance of Clay Gandy and also the soldier, who was undoubtedly Charlie Wills from the old Gandy gang.

"And what about that son of a bitch Dancer!" Quimby was now saying. "How the hell did *he* suddenly appear, busting into this place ready to tree the town!" The Judge was referring to the long, thin, liquored man whom Hames had pistol-whipped and then had carted off to jail. "What are you going to do with him? Shit, I thought the son of a bitch was in the pen."

"He was," Hames said. "And don't worry about Dancer, he'll be taken care of."

"The goddamn Gandy–Dancer gang suddenly coming back to life right here in Cracker Creek when we do *not* need it. We got too much on our plates already!" the Judge went on.

"He looked different, all duded up," Hames remarked.

"Who?"

"Gandy. Hell, he always dressed up like a tinhorn," snorted Hames. "Well, I checked the Metropole. They hadn't seen him. Seems he just got off the stage and came straight here. Like he was maybe expecting to meet... Dancer, do you reckon?"

"Maybe." Woolf Quimby inhaled into his barrel chest and then exhaled fully in realization of the drama they were experiencing.

"You think he's come back here to get that loot he stashed someplace?" the lawman asked.

"Hell, you wasn't in Cracker Creek then, Hames, but Gandy and his gang took some big hauls."

"The son of a bitch."

"He isn't no son of a bitch," said Quimby. "He's an Australian son of a bitch."

"I heard about him," Hames said, "Thinks he owns the whole world."

"Wrong again, Hames. Gandy doesn't think he owns the world; he just doesn't give a damn who owns it!" Quimby remarked. "But what happened to his grip, his bag?" he went on. "There was nothing at the Metropole."

"I checked Sol's Barber and Bath," the marshal said, "and some other places. The saloons and all."

"When he came to, he must have picked up his grip wherever he'd left it and took off. He knew Wills was dead. Likely woke up in the icehouse and found him cold as the rest of the merchandise there." A coughing laugh dropped out of the Judge's lips.

Hames picked up on the gallows humor with a tight smile. "Question is, what are we gonna do now? Anybody know the corpse ain't dead? Next to Slocum, I mean."

"I don't believe so. And it don't matter all that much."

"Anybody know about Dancer?"

"Bound to be someone," said Quimby.

"What about Slocum?"

"Maybe he had a notion about Wills, I dunno."

"We might have to take care of Slocum," the marshal observed.

"Not yet. I've got him looking into something for me. When that's done we can handle him."

Clyde Hames stood up, and from the height of his five feet, five inches looked across at the man who was still seated on the other side of the table. "I think there will come a time when a confrontation with Slocum will be necessary," he said in his formal way.

Quimby leaned forward, stifling his irritation. Hames was such a stuffed shirt! But he was good with that gun. Damn good. And Woolf Quimby needed him.

"We'll see how she blows," Quimby said easily, glad to have recovered his leadership after his unnecessary display of temper.

When the marshal closed the door behind him, Quimby was smiling. He was expecting other company, and Hames had left just in time.

"Well, my dear, I'm so glad you like it." Woolf Quimby was holding her hand as she admired the new bracelet he had bought her.

"It's lovely." Dottie's eyes were sparkling. "Oh, it is so lovely!" She held her arm out in front of her and turned it to catch the light in the colored stones. "That must have cost you a small fortune, my dear."

"Whatever it cost was not equal to one of your fingers, my dear." He was beaming, puffing a little as he stepped closer, careful though because of his great size compared to her, and because once in a similar situation he had stepped on her foot.

She was ecstatic over the gift. "You always spoil me," she said. "But please don't stop!"

Woolf Quimby, reduced to putty, giggled with unabashed joy. His whole body thrilled as she took his hand and kissed it.

"Thank you, thank you so much, dear Wolfie!"

He loved it when she called him "Wolfie." He beamed; he felt the perspiration at the back of his neck. His hands were also perspiring a little.

Suddenly he placed his big arm around her waist and she jumped.

"Forgive me, my dear." He drew back quickly in embarrassment, almost tripping as he did so. "Forgive me. I forgot myself. Your great beauty... it overcame me. I apologize."

She was slightly flushed, but recovered instantly, and standing up on her toes pecked him on the cheek. "Dear Wolfie! Thank you so much for the lovely, lovely bracelet, and all the other lovely things you've given me!"

In the next moment she was gone, leaving behind her the aroma of her perfume, which did nothing to ease the erection that was pushing harder than ever at his trousers. It was, he told himself, a great suffering, but he was madly in love with the girl. This, however, did nothing to mitigate his problem. All the same, Woolf Quimby was a man who knew how to cover his bets.

Fifteen minutes later he was untying Tony Mandell's long black hair and letting it spill onto his naked erection as he sat on the edge of his chair.

"How do you want it?" the girl asked as she bent closer to him.

"The usual," he said. "I just like it best with your hair down." She took his hard organ into her eager mouth.

To the rider's vision, the long view over the plain seemed to shimmer, and perspective was deceiving. But he knew he and the horse were well protected, indistinguishable from the big clump of willows. Only in movement, as they rode into the horizon, did they become clear to anyone who might have been looking.

They moved slowly, the horse tossing his head some, the rider watching carefully for sign, noting the eagle striking through the high sky, regal and alone. The rider's long body sharpened. Shifting in his dark brown saddle, he eased himself a bit sorely, moved the .45 at his right hip, and briefly touched the hideout gun beneath his white shirt, like he'd been crossing himself. Yet he didn't alter the slow, picking gate of the blue roan.

In a few moments he was in cover again, and he drew rein. Suddenly a jay plunged out of a stand of box elders near the creek and he watched it through the trees as it creased the sky. Then he spotted the coyote running, wondering if that was the reason for the bird's sudden flight. Or was it something else? Finally, he figured he was safe enough and he took a cheroot from the pocket of his shirt and lighted it, striking the wooden lucifer on the saddlehorn. But he didn't throw the match; he put it into the pocket of his long coat.

Seen in more detail now, he was a lean man of medium height in his middle forties, with lines of experience in his handsome face. His blue eyes were widely spaced, shaded under the brim of the plug hat with the bullet holes front and back. He reached up now and touched his full black mustache, and the dark lump on the side of his face. Then he crossed his arms, leaning forward onto the pommel of his saddle, peering out from the protection of the thin trees to study the trail ahead, and the dozen or so bareback riders who were crossing it from the east a good distance ahead. He was still feeling weak.

He counted twelve warriors as he felt the nervous chill go through him while noting that they appeared to be carrying rifles. He looked at the sky. The sun was starting to reach the horizon, and it would soon be night. He supposed it would be best to stay where he was and not try to find his destination in the dark. Certainly not with hostile Indians about. He could try again in the morning. He only hoped he could remember the location clearly.

God, prison had hurt him if he was that slow. By God, he had to be sharp. And he was cursing, of course—ah yes!—it had been the girl. Again he saw the picture on the mirror. It was on account of the girl he'd let his guard down.

That big fat son of a bitch with the bungstarter. Well, he hoped he would get another chance at the bastard. Except that he had to keep cool now. Revenge wasn't the point; the point was they just might come after him. And Wills was dead. He was on his own, and there was tomorrow to deal with.

Long Dog led his small band of warriors up the long, sloping coulee, heading toward a stand of pine and spruce just under the rimrocks. From here he could sweep the long, wide valley with the white man's glasses. They had just narrowly avoided contact with a company of mounted soldiers on the North Platte Wagon Road. He was glad for the respite. Though he hated the blue legs and wished more than anything to kill them and drive them out of their country, he also realized fully the whites' superiority in numbers and in firepower. He wondered if the horse soldiers were out looking for them, for the ones who had raided the settlers at the far end of the valley where there was the narrow creek feeding into the river. He thought they had covered their tracks carefully. But even so, he could see that his warriors were not happy. They had counted no coup, they were hungry, and no others had come out from Buffalo Horse's band to join them.

They made camp now in the stand of timber. It was a good site, well protected and with every approach visible. It had been a long, hard ride and now the braves were resting, some smoking, others having fallen asleep.

Long Dog knew he must not sleep. He had to stay awake, and he had to think. Presently, his cousin Coyote joined him and they began to discuss what needed to be done.

Beneath them, stretching as far as the eye could see, lay the great valley. In the noon light the colors of the land were myriad and brilliant, the valley winding down to the plain from which they had come, with the river flashing through the trees that lined its banks. Above them and across the valley rose the silent, eternal rimrocks as far as the soldier-glasses could see. A band of geese suddenly crossed the light blue sky above their heads.

Coyote said, "White Painted Flower is not well. She has trouble keeping up."

Long Dog nodded. "I saw this. It is from the falling from her horse at Cross Creek. But she does not cry. She is strong."

"But she can slow us if the pony soldiers come because of the firing at Cross Creek," Coyote said.

"Let us see what happens."

"We will have to leave her."

"No," Long Dog said.

"You are foolish, cousin. It is not safe to travel with someone who will make us slow and make us be caught by the soldiers. And I am seeing that we should return to Buffalo Horse. We are so few; but twelve. What can we do against the whites?"

Anger flashed into Long Dog's dark eyes. "You are a woman, Coyote!"

Coyote, who was Long Dog's favorite cousin, said, "No. I speak what is in my heart. Believe me, I wish to return to Buffalo Horse. And so do the others."

Long Dog's face darkened even more. "What others? Who wishes to return to a life of... what? Prisoners. Prisoners on our own land! Who wishes that?"

But in his heart Long Dog knew that what his cousin said was true. He knew it, for he had been fearing just this very moment when someone would voice their failure to find their freedom. Yet he could not say it. The words were not there for him to speak; yet it was in his heart, running thickly now in his blood. He knew that Coyote spoke what was true.

He looked down the slope to the shade of a tree where White Painted Flower was resting, leaning against the cottonwood. She was very fair, and beautiful. Suddenly he felt his desire for her again. But he resisted it. He knew it was no time for being with a woman; not this day with the soldiers so near. No. It was time to decide, to see what had to be done. And, yes, to listen at least to Coyote's stern words.

SLOCUM AND THE CRACKER CREEK KILLERS 93

"They will come after us," Coyote said. "The soldiers. If not now, then soon. They always come after us."

"We can ambush them," Long Dog said. He looked over at his cousin, seeing that his eyes were closed. He was not listening to him. It was not a good sign. He was losing his authority. He knew it was inevitable.

"We must go back. We must return to Buffalo Horse," Coyote said. "The soldiers will have found the one we killed by the big rocks, and they will be coming after us. The man with the big gun will have told them."

"They have not come for the white woman," Long Dog pointed out.

"They will," Coyote said.

Long Dog looked out across the gleaming valley. Never had his heart felt so heavy. Yet he knew Coyote was right.

Finally he spoke. "Let us smoke then," he said. "We will go back. But what we do now must be done well."

In the high meadow, in the stillness of the falling evening, Slocum had made camp. He was in no hurry to reach Buffalo Horse's village. First he wanted to sort out some of the things that had been happening, so he had ridden without haste, indeed carefully, as was his habit under any circumstances.

And all at once he had come upon the meadow, at the end of the long, narrow trail that wound up to the massive rimrocks, breaking through the thick growth of timber into the small, brilliant green with the dying light of the day whispering through the leaves and pine needles like a secret.

It was as good as the Sweetwater, he was thinking as he stripped his pony and hobbled him so he could feed freely on the lush grass. Then he spread his bedroll, built a small, careful fire, and cooked up some coffee and supper.

He sat near the edge of the trees, his eyes on the horse, watching him for any sign that would indicate an unwelcome visitor's approach.

He had seen the Indians earlier in the day, but since then only elk, mule deer, and a small herd of pronghorn antelope. Now he sat listening, breathing the air, which already had the quality of night in it.

He had not told Quimby that he was heading for Buffalo Horse's camp. No point in getting the man's hopes started. Anyway, he didn't trust Quimby. Quimby knew something —maybe a lot—more about Gandy than he was letting on. It seemed sure now that Gandy had come to Cracker Creek to pick up his hidden loot, planning evidently to meet up with Charlie Wills, who would probably help him. And it seemed likely too that the map was a map of the location of the bandit cache.

Was Quimby also interested in the cache? Was it that big? It seemed so. Even allowing for the usual exaggerations that always attended outlaw loot, Slocum realized the hidden cache was bound to attract more than a few.

It was obvious to him now that Quimby had intended killing Gandy not because of his remark about Eva Ronbari, but because of the loot. Only it didn't make sense. Quimby couldn't have known where the loot was, so he would have needed Gandy to lead him to it somehow. After all, he didn't get his hands on the map until after he'd clobbered Gandy.

Well, it was not Slocum's business. Quimby had hired him to get his daughter back, or at least find out what had happened to her. That was number one. The Gandy situation was just something that he'd been witness to—the death of Charlie Wills, the near-killing of Clay Gandy.

But what about the girl Dottie? He couldn't help but feel that Quimby knew about her visiting him at the Metropole. And Pony, the cigar-smoking brunette? Slocum found himself back again at the question that would not clarify itself —the feeling, really, that while Woolf Quimby wanted him to find his daughter Felicia, there was at the same time something he did *not* want him to find out. The question then was whether whatever Quimby wanted to keep hidden related directly to Felicia or himself, or both.

Now he suddenly asked himself the question as to whether any of the action he was getting more involved in had anything to do with the Golden Pig. It was a wild thought and had come unbidden from somewhere. He had no idea why. But he kept it. In any event, Woolf Quimby was a man of many parts.

As he sat on his bedroll listening to the night falling into the tall timber and the meadow, he thought how Quimby was very definitely trying to use him for something.

7

The long, thin man heard the key in the lock and was slowly alert. His head felt as though it would break into pieces.

"Dancer!"

He rolled over on the blanket which was his bedding on the hard ground that was the floor of the Cracker Creek jail, and slitted his eyes open. Further pain shot through him as his eyes met the light of the coal-oil lamp that the marshal was holding in his left hand.

"Dancer, get up. I want to talk to you."

The man on the blanket grunted and covered his eyes with his forearm. The next thing he knew pain cut through him as the marshal's boot drove into his ribs.

"I said get up, you son of a bitch!"

Anger fought with his splitting head and the pain in his side now as he rose to his knees.

98   JAKE LOGAN

"If I had my gun I'd blow the shit out of you, Hames!" And he fell as the blow hit him on the side of his head.

"Get up! Stand up!" Marshal Clyde Hames spat out the words as though tasting something very bad.

"What the hell did you hit me with yer pistol fer!" said the thin man as he struggled to his feet. "You like to broke my head!"

"You're lucky I didn't kill you, you asshole. Bustin' into the place like that, drunk as a piss-owl, running off the mouth like that!" The marshal was red with anger, but now, having said his piece, he calmed down, though with no slackening of severity in his stance. His tone was philosophical. "You're a fool, Dancer. And Quimby's sick of you."

"You can tell Quimby *I* am sick of *him*. If it wasn't for me neither of you would even *know* about Gandy's cache!"

"You're lucky Quimby doesn't get rid of you."

"He's lucky I don't get rid of him."

"That's the booze talking." The marshal's eyes closed now as he searched his memory. Then, his stance changing slightly for the delivery, his voice measured, he spoke: "The first draught a man drinks ought to be for thirst, the second for nourishment, the third for pleasure, and the fourth for madness." He opened his eyes. "Think I got it right. That was said by some old Greek."

Dancer merely snorted.

"But you, Dancer, had a good damn bit more than four drinks when you hit the Cut-And-Run," Hames went on. "You fool! Know that drink will upset the whole plan, and will likely get you a permanent home in Cracker Creek. If Quimby doesn't kill you, I will. You are a risk! Damn you, last night you just about gave the whole thing away!"

"You boys just better remember I'm your ticket to wealth."

"Only when you find that loot. Now, with Gandy about, what are you going to do?"

"I dunno." He sniffed. "I'll fix him. I'll fix the son of a bitch. But first we got to find that cache."

"God dammit, you told me an' Quimby you knew where it was."

"I do, in general, but not the detail. I got to see the place again. It's been a long time."

"Maybe there's a map," Hames said carefully, remembering the paper found in Gandy's pocket.

"You didn't know Gandy, either of you."

"What's that got to do with it?"

"Only if you'd known the son of a bitch, you'd know he never would make a map of something, or write anything down. He never put anything down that somebody else could handle." Suddenly he began to cough, but since this almost took the top of his head off, he was soon lying on the bed, trying to stifle his cough and at the same time clutching his pounding head.

Clyde Hames waited. Quimby had wanted Dancer killed, but he had argued him out of it. True, he'd pointed out, the man was a risk. But he claimed to be able to find the loot, once he got out on the trail and memory came back to him. He had been in the pen at the same time as Gandy, but had escaped a week earlier and turned up in Cracker Creek where Hames had recognized him. No one else had, not even Quimby. For this Hames took credit. He had reminded Quimby of this coup only recently, and unfortunately had reddened all over his face and neck as he did so. It had infuriated him to see the look on Quimby's face as he'd viewed the marshal's discomfort.

Thinking of this now, while waiting for Dancer to recover himself, Clyde Hames was glad Quimby had agreed finally to let Dancer live. Because now, with Gandy in the country, they would need all the help they could round up. Even Slocum, about whom Hames had had high doubts, not wanting Quimby to hire him.

But Quimby had pointed out that with Slocum already half involved with Charlie Wills's death, and having reported that the Indians who had killed him looked like a renegade band of Shoshone, it was better to have him working for them than for himself or somebody else. And maybe that was right, the marshal was now thinking. Maybe.

Dancer had stopped coughing, and now he sat up, his face and neck red, his ear cauliflowered from the barrel of Hames's Colt, his hands shaking. "Christ, Hames, get me a drink."

"Ah, Dancer, 'What the sober man has in his heart, the drunken man has on his lips!'"

"Fer Christ sake, Hames, don't pour me that bullshit, pour me a drink."

But the marshal had already left the cabin. He was back in a moment with a glass of whiskey.

"I keep this on hand, Dancer, for just such emergencies. Restorative, medicinal; but in measure, Dancer, in measure!" And he handed the glass to the shaking man, who grabbed it eagerly with both hands and drank.

"Now then, Dancer. This is the way it's going to be."

"I'll be careful next time, Hames," Dancer promised.

"No, my friend. You're not going to be careful next time."

Dancer suddenly went ash-white. "What do you mean?"

"There isn't going to be a next time. Just remember that, Dancer."

"Let me have just one more."

"One!" Hames poured.

"By God, I mind it when me an' Gandy was whipsawing this whole country, Hames. An' here I am—Dancer—begging for a fuckin' drink from a fuckin' lawman! Shit!"

"You got another name, Dancer? A first name, like?"

"Just Dancer. That's all anybody ever called me—Ma, Paw, everybody. A man don't need more'n one name. When they heard the name Dancer in the old days they shit themselves."

"Now what do they do, Dancer? They laugh."

"You go piss up a rope, Hames. You couldn't carry my cartridge belt in the old days." He paused briefly to spit boldly on the floor, not far from the marshal's shiny boots. "Nor could that son of a bitch Gandy."

"Heard he double-crossed you, Dancer."

"You heard correct. And when I catch up with that bastard I'm going to ventilate him at the right height."

"That chance might come sooner than you think, Dancer," the marshal said slyly. His face reddened and he wondered why he was reddening. And the more he wondered and got angry over it, the redder he got.

Dancer was watching him. "You got somethin' the matter with you, Hames?"

"I am telling you that you might get the chance to even it with Gandy. We'll see if you behave yourself. Tomorrow I'll turn you loose. I want you to find Gandy."

"And kill him." Dancer was nodding with each word of the marshal's.

"No. You don't kill him—not yet. You let me know where he is. That is important. You understand that?"

"I got it."

"And, by God, you stay clear of the whiskey. I even hear of you drinking anything you're a dead bird!"

He was standing right in front of the former bandit king, his eyes boring into him like bullets. "You got it, Dancer. This is the way it's going to be. You locate Gandy, you don't touch him, and you report to me."

"Or Quimby."

"You report to *me*, Dancer. To me!"

He had tilted the plug hat onto the back of his head as he struck a wooden lucifer on his thumbnail and lighted a fresh cheroot. He had seen the army patrol riding away from the herd, and wondered if they had left men behind. He could check that later, toward evening, when the light would be more in his favor.

He drew slowly on the cheroot, savoring it. It had been a long wait once he'd found the herd, but he'd had good luck finding it. But he would have wished to stay longer in the town, getting some decent food and drink, not to mention the girls and the cards. But he was living off the land now, and while that wasn't as good as being in town, it sure was a whole lot better than the pen. At any rate, he had more or less guessed his way to the Texas herd, and it was satisfying to find he'd been right.

He leaned back in the saddle now, his hand automatically reaching to his shirt pocket, only the deck of cards was not there. He spat as his horse ducked its head to feed again.

He had decided that he would settle some scores before he rode out to his destination. It had been a real surprise to discover that Leatherbee was in town, not to mention Dancer. Well, it was easy enough to figure out what they were after. Clearly, they'd heard he'd busted out of the pen. And they were coming to get their share. The damn fools, to even think that he was going to share anything with them after what he'd been through. Just like Charlie. That dumb clown, hiding out in the army like that, thinking that the time had come for him to live on easy street. It had been a surprise to see him lying there next to him in that goddamn icehouse. He shifted his weight. His head was still aching.

Christ, that fat son of a bitch had hit him with that thing! Lucky. Boy, he had been lucky. He couldn't afford another near miss like that. From now on there had to be no mistakes.

He had seen Leatherbee down there as he rode off from the herd. Going to town, maybe? The fool always was a sucker for cards and women. Well, he might have a surprise or two for him when he got back from the cards and the cribs. He looked again at the sky. It had rained during the day but now it was fairing off. Evening coming on. By God, no reason why he couldn't pull it off. The very audacity of it was what appealed to him. He had always taken risks. It was the only way. People expected certain things, certain ways of doing things, and so he had always gone them better than that. Done the thing faster, sooner instead of later, repeated it when it was thought once had been it, always throwing the other party into surprise. It was the way he liked to do things. The best, the only way, by God. It was what had gotten him to the top. And this was going to be the big one, the one they'd all remember, maybe forever.

He kicked the pony forward and started out of the trees, edging his way slowly down toward the herd of cattle, but always keeping himself just inside the cover of the trees. In this he was lucky. But luck, he knew, always favored the bold. It had always favored him, except for that time at Harlan's Crossing when he'd been taken. But that had been Dancer's double-cross, and it had been the end of the Gandy–Dancer gang. All to the good. He could look back on it quietly now that it was over and he'd gotten out of the pen. Hell, he'd even busted out of an Oregon boot, and nobody—nobody!—had ever done that. These thoughts were at the back of his mind as he rode closer to the herd.

It was darker now, with the chill in the air, the smell of water too, and good clean grass, as he rode slowly out of the clump of box elders toward the cowboy lounging in his saddle at the edge of the cattle herd.

"Howdy."

Looking up, the young drover greeted the approaching rider with a nod, revealing the customary wary neutrality of the frontier.

"Heading toward the Snake," Gandy said, studying the young cowpoke for any hostility as he reached into his pocket for a cheroot. "Got a light, have you?"

The cowboy, wearing a dusty black Stetson with a very wide brim bent downward in the front, bent his head slightly as he reached to his shirt pocket for a lucifer.

Clay Gandy slammed the barrel of his Navy Colt right along the back of that bent head. Then, grabbing the limp figure so he wouldn't fall out of the saddle, he led the cowboy's horse back into the stand of trees. He had a moment when he thought his own horse was going to spook, but it didn't. The moment passed and they made it to the spot he had in mind. There he released the unconscious cowhand, who fell to the ground.

Gandy dismounted, and with pigging strips and the

drover's own lariat he bound him, then gagged him with a piece he cut from his hickory shirt.

He mounted the cowboy's horse and led his own pony deeper into the box elders and picketed him. Then he rode back to where he had encountered the cow waddie. There was no one in sight. Good enough. He waited a moment to see if anyone would appear. But there was no one, and by now it was dark.

He had counted the men who had ridden out with Tex Leatherbee and reckoned there were four left with the herd. If he could take them, he could pull it off. If he could take them at gunpoint, one by one during the night, he could make an interesting welcome-home party for Mr. Tex Leatherbee.

It shouldn't be too difficult. He was back in form. He certainly wouldn't make another mistake like he'd done with the fat bartender and the bungstarter.

Clay Gandy grinned into the starry night. He had taken the floppy Stetson from the young cowboy and was now wearing it. And to add to his good luck, the man he had knocked out had a Winchester .44-.40 in his saddle boot.

The next morning Slocum ate a hard, dry breakfast and saddled the pony. After rubbing out all sign of his campsite, he rode out in the direction in which he had seen the Indian band the day before. He had made his decision to see if it was the same band that had attacked and killed Charlie Wills. If so, and if the girl was with the band, he would have something more firm to talk about when he met Buffalo Horse.

Halfway through the forenoon he was riding up a long mountain flank of spruce and pine when his danger sense called him. At once he drew rein and checked his bearings.

First of all, he was on a strange trail, and he was well aware of the fact that all redmen of the plains were expert in ambushing. Countless immigrant trains bore testimony to this sad statement. He knew the band of Indians he had seen the day before had also seen him, but they had been heading in another direction than his, and he had ridden carefully all through the day to make sure no one had cut his trail. Of course, this could be something else, for he had slept half awake during the night, with his horse saddled again and ready for a fast ride if necessary, and there had been nothing to cause him alarm. And so, either this was something quite new, or it was the Indian band of yesterday which had doubled back and decided to lay an ambush for him.

Turning now, he rode back down the trail at a fast canter. After about three hundred yards, he left the game trail he had switched to and headed for a bluff from where he hoped to be able to sweep a wide area with his field glasses.

He was disappointed. Yet he waited, seeing no sign of an enemy. He waited and listened. Suddenly his spotted horse lifted his ears in the direction from which they had just ridden. Slocum wondered what had warned him.

There were many things in the world of nature that could signal warnings of varying sorts, birds of all kinds, and little ground animals, and there were sounds and smells and subtle feelings. Something had told him that there was an enemy near. Quickly he planned his strategy.

He had a fast horse and now turned him and sped back down the trail and took a fresh turning. He was looking for a hill with a jutting ledge, a place where he could dismount and be above anyone tracking him and thus have the advantage.

Presently he saw such a place as the trail fed around a hill and led right to a tight stand of trees. He galloped his horse off the trail and then dismounted and led him about a hundred yards into the timber. He groundhitched his lathered mount, then hurried forward and waited behind a tree with his eyes on his back trail. But nothing came in sight. He didn't wait very long, satisfied now that he wasn't going to see any Indian at that point.

Now he hurried through the timber and on up the hill, dropping to his hands and knees at the top and crawling forward to a bluff above the trail. From here he had a clear view down.

About two hundred yards down the trail he saw the band of about fifteen warriors riding slowly, obviously following his trail. Somewhere near the middle he saw the flaxen hair, the bare legs of the woman. She was riding a tall sorrel.

Slocum knew how easily he could have shot at least three of them from where he was, but he held his fire, not sure whether the Indians might not kill the girl immediately. He could see her more closely now. She was dressed Indian fashion, but this did not conceal a full womanly figure. Quimby had described his daughter, and from what he had told him, Slocum was sure this was Felicia.

They were moving slowly, wary of the trail, so he had time to study the girl. She was obviously in good standing with the group of Shoshone, riding well, with her head high, her hands free. There was nothing in her bearing or in the way the Shoshone seemed to behave toward her that would suggest she was a miserable prisoner. It occurred to Slocum that the girl might have chosen to stay with them, if she had been offered any choice. Maybe she was just making the best of it. It was impossible to tell. All he could tell Quimby would be that Felicia certainly didn't give the appearance of having been mistreated. She looked well fed, and carried herself with a dignity matched by her captors. It was obvious to Slocum that the girl had been accepted as part of the band. What her feelings were on the subject of her captivity, willing or not, he had no way of telling.

By now the lead warrior was abreast of him. It would be only moments before they reached the place where he had left the trail. He was reasonably sure they wouldn't spot what he had done and would ride past the place where he had started up the hill. The ground was hard and rocky and he hoped it wouldn't occur to them that he would pull such a trick as he had; that instead they would figure he had ridden on ahead. The only question was how far ahead would the trail by itself hide the fact that he had left it. Soon enough it would leave the hard rock and once again becoming earth would reveal the fact that he had fooled them.

The girl was in full view now and he saw that she was indeed beautiful, though bearing no resemblance that he could see to Quimby. Perhaps she was like her mother. He wondered if the Shoshone felt that her long yellow hair was something special. He wondered too who her man was, or whether all of them were.

There was no time to waste now. He crawled back to his horse, mounted, and started down the other side of the hill. Part of the way down he dismounted and led the horse, for the trail had become steep and he was afraid of dislodging stones that would signal his whereabouts.

He made it safely to the flat tableland below, but just as he did so a cry broke out from above. Looking up, he saw a warrior waving to others behind him. Shots followed immediately as he kicked his horse into a fast gallop.

Woolf Quimby was an early riser. He lived in a large house with his wife and fourteen children at the edge of town. Rising at pre-dawn, he would be the first up. He liked it that way. Nobody was around to ask him anything, and he could savor the fresh air of the day, and plan. He dearly loved to plan. After all, seeing himself in the role of patriarch, not only to his own brood but to all of Cracker Creek as well, he knew it was necessary to plan, to encourage and avoid as the case might be, and to dispense justice. Solomon and Socrates were his models, though he had never read a word of either. In fact, the Judge seldom read, not being very able at the exercise. His formal schooling had been limited. His parents had been wiped out in a flash flood when he was still a shaver, as he would put it when asked. A shaver, but one who had a quick learning ability. Like many young shavers he learned how to manipulate the non-shavers, the elders. And from that point on his career was set. It was only to be expected that he would inhabit the various roles and offices which he now wore with such ease, and even grace, as some of his more obsequious partisans had observed.

This morning he put out the numerous cats who had stolen into the house during the night, brewed coffee, and carried it out to his woodshed, where he ensconced himself with a cigar and his thoughts. The latter consisted of plans for the resuscitation not only of the Golden Pig but, unknown to the other members of the council, the other failed mines as well, the capture of the Gandy–Dancer cache, and the retrieval of his favorite daughter Felicia. These were the three prongs of his earthly, or immediate, plan.

Over all of this lay the beaming ray of his undying love. And here too the Judge had exercised thorough practicality. For it wasn't realistic to love the great Eva Ronbari without being able to worship her carnally as well. Since this was physically impossible—after all, he'd never so much as laid eyes on her in person—he had solved the impossible by making his great "love" a reality through the form of Dottie Finlightly. True, the carnal favors coming from Dottie were infrequent. Still, the lack of satiation—if that were at all possible, and he doubted it—yet kept his passion at a peak, and gave him the edge he needed for a life that would otherwise have been dull, dreary, and drab. Then, too, he had had the presence of mind to acquire the sexual allegiance of the delightful Tony. Since he kept the gorgeous Tony well oiled with lucre, she made herself available at any time, any place.

Woolf had only been in his woodshed for perhaps half an hour, polishing his thoughts and enjoying his coffee and cigar, when he heard the horse approaching—the snort, the jingle of the bit, and the creak of leather. A heavy man. He knew who it was, yet he didn't ever take chances—except those times when he did lose his temper with Gandy and again with Hames. So he rose and went to the window. Quietly he watched Clyde Hames riding up on a tough little dun gelding and, with a loud creaking of leather, dismount. Stolid as a bear, the marshal of Cracker Creek approached the door of the woodshed and knocked. Quimby intentionally allowed him this action, rather than opening the door before he got there to greet him, in order to maintain the necessary distance between himself and his law enforcer.

The Judge had brought the coffee pot and an extra mug with him. Now, seating himself, nodding toward a second chair, he raised his eyebrows at his visitor. "Jawbreaker?"

SLOCUM AND THE CRACKER CREEK KILLERS 111

Clyde Hames nodded. He sat down, sighing, still a little sleepy. It was just getting to be dawn now. He liked these occasional early morning meetings in the woodshed. It was away from any interruption and he liked the smell of the chopped wood. He even liked the desk with Quimby's papers spilling all over it. It was far better than the lonely room he had in the Widow O'Shea's house. Clyde Hames had a yearning for domesticity, but had met no one to fulfill the other half of his longing since his wife Caddy had died shortly after their marriage. It had happened during a drunken brawl in the town they were living in, when a stray bullet fired by one of the outlaws had felled her. She'd been wounded, which killed the possibility of Hames mounting instant reprisal against the villain, for he remained to nurse his wife, who didn't die for nearly a week. By then, Hames was a wall of vengeance, and not only dealt with the miscreant by killing him, but also wiped out a few of his buddies.

Clyde had been pretty much of a sport himself until the terrible episode. Since that time he had become the symbol of rectitude, the role in which Cracker Creek knew him Sometimes the object of laughter and even ridicule—behind his back, of course—he was always respected as a man of honesty and remorseless justice.

It was one of the brilliant observations of Woolf Quimby that realized Clyde Hames had another side. The cutup and hellraiser in him hadn't been totally killed. Quimby had early seen that the man was honest as the day was long, as the saying had it, but there *was* the night. Like everyone, in Quimby's book, he could be bought. The bait was simple, and the oldest in the book: Tony.

Seating himself with a grunt now, Hames took the cigar and coffee Quimby offered and settled back in his chair, which creaked and even spread its legs dangerously under his great weight.

"Better watch that seat," Quimby muttered. He was no lightweight himself.

Hames sat in rebellious immobility, silently sipping his coffee, for it was still hot, and his lips were sore from Tony chewing on them, as Quimby's sharp eyes had instantly observed.

"What's with Dancer?" the Judge asked, speaking around his large cigar. And he took the cigar out of his mouth, as though to listen better.

"He'll be all right," Hames said. "I think he's got scared."

"He had damn well better be."

"The booze will kill him if a dose of lead don't."

Quimby regarded the man opposite him, thinking how he truly symbolized the solidity of the law and justice. Hames sat there solid as a new wagon box. And not a hell of a lot more intelligent, his host was reflecting.

"So he doesn't know exactly where the cache is, or so he says," Quimby remarked. "But he's still saying he can lead us to it. That right?"

"That is correct."

"When?"

"Whenever we say. Whenever *you* say." Hames's broad, stolid face was as innocent as the face of an ox.

Quimby, however, knew better. He didn't trust anybody. Probably he wouldn't have trusted Eva Ronbari in his present mood.

"Does he know I've got the map?"

Hames shook his big head. "No. But you know that map don't say much."

"It might to Dancer."

"Dancer claims he wasn't actually with Gandy when the money box was hidden. But he knows the area. But he has to see it. It's been a while." And then he added, "He says."

"The son of a bitch. He's sober now, is he?"

"Sober and ready. I told him I would kill him slowly if he screwed up. Not only that, he said that Gandy would never have made a map except to throw somebody off. And I believe that."

"I believe it too," Quimby agreed. "When there's that kind of money in it, you don't need something on paper. But up here." He tapped his forehead slowly with his thick middle finger. He leaned forward now, his big bronze eyes hard. "I want you to stay right close to Dancer. Even with him locked up in your jail there, I mean it, Hames. I am not happy about the way he got drunk and like to spilled the whole thing in the Cut-And-Run."

"He didn't say anything about the cache."

"He was sore at you, Hames. And he could have easily spilled it."

"A pity you hit Gandy so goddamn hard," Hames said, his tone hard and sour as he glared at Quimby.

Quimby didn't like it, but he had to go carefully. Hames had a temper. "I had no way of knowing he was Gandy, for Christ's sake. Did *you* know that dude was Clay Gandy? No, you didn't! So let's cut that out!" He was pleased at seeing the tide of scarlet flowing into the marshal's face.

"I'll handle Dancer," Hames said.

"I know you will. We have got to deal with the facts. And it's a fact that Clay Gandy is loose, and probably on his way to pick up the cache."

"I think you screwed up again," Hames said, defending his ground.

"What the hell do you mean, God damn it!" Quimby all but charged out of his chair, but restrained himself.

"I mean, why didn't you send someone to cut his trail after he lit out from here? That's what I mean. That's what I would have done!"

A deep breath came pumping out of Woolf Quimby's body, like air from a deflating balloon.

"You would make a good lawman, Hames, except for your lack of intelligence. I mean, you are dumb thinking I am dumb. Do you think I didn't figure that out? I have got not only somebody on his trail, but that man on his trail has got men with him—on Clay Gandy's trail!"

"Who?" demanded Hames. "Who you got?"

"Big Tex Leatherbee and a couple of his boys. That's who. Big Tex, who rode with Gandy in the old days. Knows him! And who's now running cattle. He's working for me now!"

And Clyde Hames, his whole face and neck almost the color of mahogany, such was his embarrassment, sat there looking at his tormentor as he realized how again he had put his foot in it.

Now in the Shoshone camp there was no laughter, no games among the children; the young boys were not throwing mud balls with the yellow sticks, not playing the war game of Throwing Them Off Their Horses where one boy would be a horse and a smaller boy the warrior rider who would grapple with another horse and rider.

In Buffalo Horse's lodge the chief sat with Long Dog and Coyote, who had ridden in that morning.

"What is it you have come for, Long Dog?" Buffalo Horse asked, looking at the young warrior seated across from him.

"Coyote and myself have been fighting with the white people since we left your lodge," Long Dog said.

"That I know. And you have caused much to sadden the hearts of our people," the chief said. "Tell me why you have come."

"We have come to ask your help, Grandfather," Long Dog said. "For all my life you have taught us many things, ever since we were small children, myself and my cousin Coyote. We owe you much, and now we are asking you to help us." Long Dog looked at his cousin sitting beside him. "We have fought the whites, but we cannot defeat them. There are too many of them."

"The soldier men are looking for you," Buffalo Horse said. "You want me to hide you. How can I do this when you have disobeyed your elders?" The chief spoke with no expression on his lined face. "I have heard much of your fighting."

"But it was we who were often attacked by the whites."

"We spoke long ago about this," Buffalo Horse said. "Yet you went. We spoke of there being too many white people, more of them than there are blades of grass on the earth. We spoke of the senselessness of fighting them. You did not listen. It has always been the trouble with you both —you, Long Dog, and you, Coyote."

"But now, Grandfather," Coyote said, "now we see the truth of what you spoke to us so long ago."

"You did not think of the people when you left three winters ago and took the white woman with you."

Buffalo Horse was silent for a long time. In his heart he was not in disagreement with the young men. He could not blame them for their restlessness. Who with warrior blood in him would want to stay in this one place without hunting, without an occasional raiding party, without the freedom to come and go?

Leaning forward a little, he lifted the pipe from its special place, picked up a buffalo chip from the fire, and held it to the bowl of the pipe, drawing the smoke as he did so. Carefully he passed the pipe, and waited while the two young warriors smoked.

At last Buffalo Horse spoke. "It is that the people must survive. So that we can live and the Spirit in us can live. We are all prisoners here. On our own land. Yet we do not own the land. The land is not owned, nor the animals, nor the people. Yet, if we make war on the Wasichus we will all be killed. The women and the children will all be killed. And the men. Who will be there to remember our dead? Who will be here to live our way? We must live. The people must live so that we can remain. We must find our hearts so that we can help The Above."

He sat without moving, absolutely still, as the silence filled the lodge.

Finally the chief spoke again. "I ask you to untie your horse's tail and follow the path of peace. We are all brothers. All."

"And if the pony soldiers come for us, Grandfather—what then?"

"I do not know," Buffalo Horse said. "You do not speak truly with me, even though you have smoked the pipe. You know that when one smokes the pipe one cannot lie."

"We have not lied to you, Grandfather," Coyote insisted.

"No, you have not lied. But you have not told the truth."

The two young warriors bowed their dark heads, for it was so.

It was at this point that Buffalo Horse felt the change of atmosphere in the camp. He looked toward the flap of the tipi just as a hand appeared at its corner and opened it to admit a young warrior.

"Who is coming?" Buffalo Horse asked.

"A lone white man, mounted."

"A pony soldier?"

"It is a man who knows the land, not a soldier man. A big man, but not one from the cows, and he does not feel like one of the Gray Men."

"And he is not followed?"

"He is by himself. He has asked to see Buffalo Horse. He is called Slow Come."

8

The storm started around the middle of the night with a sudden and totally unexpected driving wind from the north and west. It swept over the land, battering everything in its path with a cold sleet that cut to the bone of the men on night herd. Then the wind slackened and the sleet turned to a cold, drizzling, steady rain that soaked into everything. Close to dawn it stopped, and as the sun rose above the horizon the land welcomed it, emitting little plumes of steam as the warmth met the cold and wet left by the departed storm.

Gandy had been patient, more than patient, waiting for Tex Leatherbee and his two cowboys to return from town. He had cut down the four other men watching the herd, coming up on them in more or less the same way he had taken his first rider. And fortunately he had done this after the storm, in the early dawn so that the drovers had been there to hold the herd during the night. Otherwise, his game would have been known. He sat his pony now, hidden from view as the sun rose, waiting among the dewy cottonwood trees and box elders by the creek. Relaxing just a little—carefully not too much—he took out a small cigar and lighted it. He wore the young cowboy's hat, turned down to hide his face should anyone come upon him suddenly, and he wore his slicker. He was well disguised and at the same time ready to move in closer to the herd if necessary should anyone ride by to wonder what he was doing there.

He did feel tired. He was an older man now, after those years in the pen. And he was tired. But he kept his vigilance; he didn't slacken off the way a younger man might have. He had been too long on the owlhoot trail to forget that caution. The side of his head still hurt where he'd been slugged with the bungstarter. Even his thoughts felt tired at that moment.

It had been a long ride from Laramie. And strange. Not at all what he had imagined in his anticipation. But God, it was good to be out. So many things were coming back. The smells, the taste of the high air, the tall sky drawing him and at the same time enclosing him so that he felt one with it and with the earth on which he had been riding. And at night the breathing of the ground beneath him as he lay in his bedroll or sat at his fire. Those long years! And at last the freedom for which he had longed. Oh, he would have waited till his sentence was up, only Dancer had broken out. And Dancer would go for the buried cache. A small fortune there! And not so small either! Even without the loot that he'd saved over those years when the gang had ridden out on the best horseflesh and whipsawed the entire countryside, by God; even without the loot at the end of the rainbow there was the freedom! To be free! Oh, God, yes. To be free—with no fences, nothing holding you. To come and go as you felt like it. Like the Indians. Except for them it was not so any longer. They too had been caught, trapped, stuck into prison and on reservations. Not that he felt sorry for those red bastards any more than he did for any of the white sons of bitches who had foiled him. But now, with fences going up all over the big country, and the law all about, where could a man go? Well, it was free for himself. Anything was better than that goddamn prison. He could never stand that again. He never would.

He would take Leatherbee and those two who had ridden off with him, likely to town. Big Tex, he'd heard, had gone into the cattle business while himself and Dancer and Charlie were in the clink. Charlie was dead, Dancer might as well be; the bugger had always been a boozer, and he'd heard that when he got out he hadn't changed. Well, that was enough of the old gang. What luck, though! Tex Leatherbee in Cracker Creek! Had the nerve to push a herd of stolen cattle up from Texas. He knew they were stolen, for he'd taken time to inspect a few of the brands. Tex had always been good with a running iron. A small herd, but profitable.

The funny thing was him picking just this time, when he and Dancer were about. He wondered if anyone else from the old gang was about. For sure not Charlie. And he'd heard in Laramie that the Haggerty brothers, Tom and Sid had gotten shot up in North Town. And Red McLaughlin had caught too much lead holding up a train. Red had never been very bright; undoubtedly he screwed the thing up. Yes, the old days were over. Even Dancer; he'd been useful, a fair-to-good man in his day except for the drink. But toward the end, their last job which he'd messed up and they'd got the law on them—screwed up with drinking!—toward the end he was dodgey. And right now the son of a bitch wasn't worth the lead to blow him to hell.

He sat there on the cowboy's pony, his own horse being picketed in the trees, and waited, thinking over his plan, how he would get to the mine, wondering if anyone had picked up on the fake map he'd given Charlie Wills a long while ago to throw anyone off. Charlie had set himself up in the army. What a laugh! Charlie, the good-time boy, who would have liked the army like he would the piles on a McClellan saddle. But he'd stuck it out! Charlie'd been just a kid when he'd joined the gang just before they'd all got taken. But he'd proved his worth, breaking out of prison first and getting word back to him on the lay of the land. Too bad those red devils had gotten him; he was a good kid. Course, the good thing was there was less to split now. Now he had it all for himself. No split to Charlie, none to Dancer, and for sure none to Tex. He grinned. Yes, by God, it was good to be free!

J. Orville DeWitt left nothing to be desired as he greeted Woolf Quimby. He was in truly brisk form, his ebullience matched only by his vigorous and incisive diction and the flash of his humor-loving eye. Even before the Judge could state his business, J. Orville had whipped out some brown sheets of wrapping paper on which the latest edition of the *TaleTeller* was being printed and began to read:

"When an Eastern girl of tender years recently asked her mother on a visit to the Great West, 'Ma, do cowboys eat grass?' the old lady replied, 'No, dear, they're part human.' Well, the *TaleTeller* appreciates wisdom of this caliber."

SLOCUM AND THE CRACKER CREEK KILLERS 123

The editor and publisher was still cackling as his visitor accepted the proffered chair with no back, and sat down.

"I have been trying to locate John Slocum," Quimby began. "I know you and him know each other. Where the hell is he? Has he left town?"

Orville sucked his gums for a moment, a habit he had when under stress. "I have no idea where the gentleman is," he said in a loud voice, trying in this manner to put Quimby on the defensive. But it didn't work.

"I've got to find him," Quimby said.

"Is there something the *TaleTeller* can help you on?" DeWitt asked, cocking his head to one side, his long nose sniffing for news.

"No. Only that I've heard the Shoshone are getting particularly restless, as indeed they revealed with the killing of that young soldier a few days ago. I had hired Slocum to try to meet with the Shoshone chief, Buffalo Horse, to see whether or not some arrangement could be made for ransom. I've been trying for three years to get my daughter back. And the army does nothing! Yes...!" He suddenly roared. "Yes, you can do something! You can write it up in your paper what a bunch of fools the army is. They don't protect the citizens *at all,* sir! And you cannot get them to investigate a thing. Granted the tribe or band or whatever it was left the country, or so the military claims; they went beyond Fort Tyrone's jurisdiction, whatever the hell that means; still, they're now reported back in this part of the territory. The band has been shooting up livestock, running off horses, and scaring the bejesus out of good, honest settlers, sir! I want you to put that in your paper, Mr. DeWitt!"

Orville had not been at all prepared for such an onslaught of outrage, but he rallied, collected himself, and jabbed his pencil at a piece of paper, purportedly taking notes. He said he would do what he was asked. The *TaleTeller* would indeed write up the inconstancy, the inconsistency, the irresponsibility of the army. Now, while they were together, could not the Judge give him a story on the opening of the Golden Pig, and would the other shafts be drained, and how much money did they expect...? Finally Woolf Quimby rose to his feet and started for the door, unable to deal with the torrent of questions thrown at him by DeWitt.

But Orville had his reasons for such an avalanche, which was to dislodge the Judge from his usually incredibly stolid stance in the face of embarrassing questions. And he did this by suddenly saying, as Quimby was at the door, "Judge, do you have any idea at all what happened to the man who was struck with a bungstarter in the Cut-And-Run recently, was pronounced dead and put in the icehouse, and who to all intents and purposes rose from the dead, a modern-day Lazarus, and walked away. Never to be seen or heard from again."

"I have no idea who he was," Quimby said, paling.

"Do you not think it passing strange that there was nobody in town who appeared to know him, or even care what happened to him?"

"This is the frontier, Mr. DeWitt, not the powdered drawing rooms of the Eastern cities."

Quimby stepped out of the *TaleTeller* office and was about to close the door. But Orville DeWitt, swift as a magician with a highly trained rabbit, moved out onto the boardwalk with him.

The newspaperman's nose was inches away from Quimby's face as he said, "Did this passage-at-arms at the Cut-And-Run have any relation at all with the head-and-pistol encounter between Marshal Clyde Hames and the notorious former road agent named Dancer? And, sir..." With his long, rusty-looking forefinger right under Quimby's thick nose, "Did you know that one Clay Gandy, also a former road agent and a man connected in trade to the above-mentioned Dancer—sir, did you know that this man Gandy has escaped from the federal penitentiary?"

Quimby had control by now, though a shock of pain ran through him at the mention of Gandy. "I know nothing, sir. But..." He recovered himself fully now. "But I shall be pleased to read all about it in your newspaper."

And he was gone, rolling along the boardwalk at top speed. J. Orville DeWitt grinned grimly after him. He had suspected as much. He hoped, however, that he hadn't tipped his hand, for he did know where Slocum had gone; he hoped that his attack had covered his defense. But it didn't matter too much. Slocum could take care of himself as far as Quimby was concerned. Orville had no qualms there. But how he would handle Chief Buffalo Horse and his warriors was something else. DeWitt might go so far as to pray for John Slocum, though he was not a religious man, but he would certainly not wish to trade places.

He walked back into his office, thinking how he might approach Marshal Clyde Hames for a story on his famous prisoner, Dancer. At the same time, a spasm of caution suddenly entered his seventy-year-old body. He had a sudden feeling that something was going on that was a lot more than he at any rate was able to see. And while he was a fairly brave man, he was no hero. Moreover, would he be helping Slocum or hindering him by calling attention to the fact that Quimby was acting mighty funny for a man who was supposedly solely bent on the retrieval of his daughter? The possibility was at hand now for the first time in a long while, with the Shoshone renegade band back in the country.

J. Orville stood in the middle of his office, pondering. Finally he decided to do what he always did when confronted with a difficult problem. He sat down, put his feet up on the other chair, and fell asleep.

A cat had wandered into the office without his noticing. He was a buckskin-colored creature and he had been lying by the cold stove, sleeping. He often visited the office. Now, as a gargling snore rolled out of the editor's nose and mouth, the visitor raised his head, looked back at the man slumped in the big chair, and then rose silently to his feet and ran out.

It was nearly always that way whenever he approached an Indian camp, the strangest thing, this way that he felt. First of course there was the sense of care, even danger, but there was something else, something he couldn't name and had never really wished to name. It was whatever it was.

When he rode around the cutbank at Horse Creek, there it was on a low rise of ground surrounded by box elder, willow, and cottonwood. Approaching in full view as he had to since the only way was across the plain, Slocum was enthralled by the containment, the serenity of the scene before him. Even knowing that he was being escorted at some distance by the camp police, he still noted the light-and-shadow dancing of the sunlight on the thick goldenrod. At the same time, he knew how easily a man could be taken by such beauty and lose his scalp.

Yet he still felt something pulling him at the sight of the smoke rising from the lodge smoke holes, the tinkle of the grazing bells in the horse herd, and he thought for a brief moment of the barbed wire that was filling the land now.

As always he picked up on the details, knowing this was the most important, as long as you didn't get lost in them. No game was visible, nor did he see any buffalo chips. And he saw too that the bark on the trees had not been rubbed off as it used to be by the buffalo scratching themselves. One more sign of the disappearance of the great herds.

The Shoshone camp seemed unusually still. Customarily there would be much activity, a great deal of movement and laughter, the children playing and fighting too with mud balls, the bigger boys wrestling at games of war, the women sewing and washing clothes, and there would be the inevitable dogs. Now the lone dog barking as Slocum rode closer sounded a note of desolation.

As he rode closer, the warriors who had been escorting him at a distance rode nearer to him, forming a loose circle all the way around him. As they came to the village a few of the Indians who happened to be in sight stood still, staring at him with bold eyes, while others turned away. The women appeared to be carved in their immobility and silence.

Buffalo Horse was alone in his lodge when Slocum was brought in by a short, muscular warrior with a long scar down his chest. Slocum, who was well aware of the importance of Indian custom, was careful not to hurry, nor to jump to any conclusion, or assume anything at all. He was patient, he observed; like the Indian, he knew that everything was attention.

A seat had been placed opposite the chief, across from the low fire of buffalo chips. Slocum sat down. Buffalo Horse had filled the traditional pipe and now he lighted it, lifting a small chip from the fire to do so. He passed it to his visitor, and for some moments they smoked in silence.

"Now we can speak with straight words," the Shoshone chief said. "For we have smoked together."

Slocum inclined his head in a nod, remembering how few gestures the Indian sitting in front of him was making. Only the necessary, he was thinking; this had long been a value for him which he followed as he could.

"You have come about the white woman with Long Dog's band. Now that Long Dog has returned from the Smokey Basin country I have been expecting the white man and even the soldiers."

"You know too about the soldier man who was killed at Prairie Gap? I think it could have been Long Dog's band."

"You have come about that soldier? I know nothing of whether it was Long Dog," Buffalo Horse said.

"No, I came only about the woman. I mention the soldier because I was there and I saw a white woman riding off with the Shoshone warriors. There were twelve warriors. I thought it might be Long Dog."

"The soldier chief will send men about that," Buffalo Horse said. He lifted the pipe and smoked for a moment. "You have come to take the woman back to her people. But I cannot give her to you."

"Her father is in despair. He will pay a ransom for her if necessary. He will not seek revenge and he will not fight the Shoshone for this. He only wants his daughter."

"The woman is with Long Dog and his band."

"But you are the chief." Even though pointing this out, Slocum knew the answer, for he understood many things about the Indian way. It was why he had to go slowly.

"Long Dog left his people when he went to the Smokey Basin country, taking the white woman with him."

"You say he is no longer a part of your village."

The chief took another smoke before replying to Slocum. After quite a long moment he said, "Yes and no. Long Dog has been told what he must do if he wishes to return. I wait to see what he will choose. But I do not order him." Then he added without rancor, "The Shoshones are not like the whites. We do not order and demand. It is not our way."

"I know that, Buffalo Horse. I understand that."

"You will have to be patient."

"I understand that too," Slocum said. "But even so, being patient, can you advise me? Is there a way to approach Long Dog?"

"I will speak to Long Dog."

"The girl's father will pay well for her. He is rich."

The chief's eyes were looking over the top of his visitor's head. "Long Dog, if he agrees, will surely want payment, but I do not think it will be the kind of payment the father will expect." He let his words wash into a different silence now.

Slocum sat there taking in the smell of bear grease, the odors of tobacco and the small fire.

After a long moment the chief spoke. "Long Dog is angry. The whites did things to the old ones when he was little and made him watch. It will not be easy to satisfy him." He paused, his eyes deep inside himself. Then he spoke again. "Come back." He held up one finger and with his forearm made a half-circle movement from one horizon to the other. Then he did the same with two fingers, and then with three.

"I will come back in three days," Slocum said.

And the silence in which the chief was now wrapped followed him out of the lodge to where a warrior was waiting with his spotted pony.

* * *

There were fifteen of them, a few more since the fight with the pony soldier when the man with the big gun had killed Runs Away Fast and Standing Man. Except for Sign-in-the-Sky, who had known forty winters, they were all young. They had returned to their tribal ground, for the soldiers had been all over the place up at Smokey Basin and it had been difficult to hunt, and also the soldiers were looking for somebody, they had heard. Maybe it was them. It didn't matter. The soldiers killed everybody anyway, whether you had done something bad or not.

Now they were back near Buffalo Horse's people and the white woman was still with them. Long Dog had taken her for his wife and they had been together now for two winters and nearly three springs. It was good. At first she had been refusing everything, but Long Dog had been patient and had taught her and she had learned. She learned quickly. With the band on the move all the time she had to learn so.

Once, something bad happened, when Carry His Horse was looking at the white woman, White Painted Flower, and Long Dog had seen the way he looked and he had beaten Carry His Horse with his riding quirt. He had whipped Carry His Horse to his knees and then kicked him and spat upon him and ordered him away from the camp.

But then Sign-in-the-Sky, who was older, had talked to Long Dog, saying how they needed all the warriors they could get, for the band was small, and that Carry His Horse was a strong warrior, even though he had acted badly with the woman White Painted Flower. It would be better to let him stay in the band and he could help them when there was fighting.

Long Dog had not wanted to, but his cousin Coyote had

agreed with Sign-in-the-Sky, and so finally Long Dog had relented and allowed Carry His Horse back into the camp.

And so there had been trouble and this was not good. Now things were worse, for the soldier men were even near the Shoshone camp. They were always everywhere! They were looking for the ones who had wiped out the soldier at Prairie Gap, the lone soldier, and it was strange that he had been riding along all by himself. For usually the blue legs rode with others. They always did. This one had been different. Even so, it was said that the soldiers would come for revenge against the ones who had killed him. And perhaps the one with the long gun who had shot at them and killed Standing Man and Runs Away Fast had been with many soldiers and was even now looking for them.

Thus Long Dog had ridden to the camp of the Buffalo Horse people to speak and smoke with Buffalo Horse and ask if they might stay there for a while until the soldier men from the fort grew quiet or tired and went back again to their big wooden house with the high fence around it.

Now, when Long Dog returned to their camp after the talk with Buffalo Horse, all could see he was not happy. He said nothing, not even to Coyote or to Sign-in-the-Sky, but sat on his blanket and was very still. After he had been back at the camp a whole day, while all waited for him to tell what had happened, he rose and called Sign-in-the-Sky to him and asked him to help him prepare the rocks and the place for a sweat, on a certain high place that was near their present camp.

But even this was to be a disappointment, for even before they started out from camp, Red Little Man, who had been out looking for game, rode into camp fast to tell that there was a white man near. He was alone and he had one of the big guns in his saddle holder, the one the whites called Sharps. He was riding toward the place where the white men took the yellow rocks out of the ground.

"Let him go," Coyote and Sign-in-the-Sky both said, but Long Dog said no, he wanted to capture the white man, to find out what the soldier men and the other whites were doing.

And then Walks Far came riding in. He had also seen the white man and said he was the same one who had gotten away from them the other day when he had tricked them at the tall hill.

Long Dog didn't even wait to hear what Coyote or Sign-in-the-Sky had to say about that. He had already turned toward his pony and was calling out orders to the warriors who had gathered around to hear the news.

It was only a matter of moments before they had ridden out and the campsite was left to the hot sun and the heavy scent of bear grease and sage.

In the early forenoon the sky suddenly clouded over and it began to rain again. It was not like the storm of the night before, when there had been sleet and the driving northwest wind; this was less a slicing rain that cut sideways into the cattle herd than it was a straight pelting with large drops. It came down hard, and it came suddenly without any warning. For a moment Gandy thought it was going to be a flash flood, but there was no lightning, no thunder, nothing, fortunately, that would stir the cattle into stampeding, though they were definitely restless.

Not that he cared. They weren't his. Let Tex worry over that one with his near thousand head of beeves, most of them branded over with a running iron.

The drops began to get bigger and all at once the rain

stopped. Gandy had ridden to a new place where he could watch for anyone riding in. It was beginning to clear now and because he had been awake most of the night he was feeling sleepy. To keep awake he now rubbed tobacco juice into his eyes, just like any trial waddy would do.

Yes, he was tired. It had been a lot of action lately, the escape from Laramie, the ride to Cracker Creek, the action in the saloon with that big son of a bitch and his bungstarter, and now the trail again. He wished Leatherbee and his pair of cowboys would get back. It would be better doing what he planned without bright sunlight. He needed all the cover he could get.

All at once he heard the horse nicker. Off there to his right, coming in on the trail through that stand of willows. It had to be Leatherbee and the boys. Yes, two horses, maybe three. And closer now.

Clay Gandy never even felt the gun barrel that slashed down on the back of his head, nor the hard ground hitting him as he fell out of his saddle and landed flat on his back.

"You gonna shoot the son of a bitch?" one of the cowboys said.

Big Tex Leatherbee spat casually within a few inches of the unconscious man who was still wearing the floppy black Stetson.

"I hope I didn't hit him too hard," he said.

"Why not shoot the bastard?" his companion asked.

"Then who would tell me what I want to know?" Tex said, holstering his big sixgun. "And besides," he added, "I want him to know who coldcocked him and outsmarted him. The lousy son of a bitch!"

Big Tex sat his big bay horse, thinking how he had waited for this moment, and especially during the past night. All the night he had waited, for they hadn't ridden off. He had known Gandy would come, especially when Woolf Quimby had told him what had happened and had asked him to "regulate" his former leader. Tex had argued a bit, raising Quimby's price, but all along he'd been only too glad for the news that Gandy had finally made it to Cracker Creek from Laramie, and could lead him to the big prize. The only thing he didn't like was that there were a number of people in on the hunt—Dancer, Quimby, and maybe even Hames. And who else?

Anyway, Gandy was the big one. And he would show where the cache was. The question was, did Dancer also know where it was? And where the hell was Dancer? In jail, he had heard, after bracing Clyde Hames while loaded up with forty-rod. The damn fool! Had he spilled to Hames? Was Hames as much Quimby's man as everybody said?

"Shit," he muttered thoughtfully, and squinted at the sky, trying to read the weather.

"Didn't catch ya, Tex," said the cowboy standing beside him.

"I said Shit! Goddamnit to hell. Shit!"

"What I'm saying, Hames, is the quicker we get out there the better. We cannot afford to sit around here while maybe Gandy and God knows who else—because you know there could be others!—gets out there and locates you-know-what!"

"You figurin' on coming along, Quimby?" Dancer asked. He was sitting in the corner of the office in the Cut-And-Run, sitting on the floor with his bony back supported by the wall. Hames was standing, while Quimby was sitting at his desk.

"I am certainly planning to visit the site of the famous

lost treasure, Dancer. And the marshal will be there, and perhaps some men to protect us on the way back, should we need protection."

"You're talking about guns."

"I am talking about guns." The Judge nodded in full agreement, his big head rolling forward on his chest and shoulders, slightly awkwardly like a toy that wasn't quite working having had too much rough handling by the children.

"So when are we leaving?" Dancer asked. He sniffed, screwing up his lean, hungry-looking face, and then rubbing his nose with the back of his wrist.

"We'll be leaving this afternoon," Quimby said. "We would have left earlier, but we had to wait for you to sober up,"

"Boy, I could use a drink, Judge."

"You shit," Hames said in disgust.

"There will be no liquor forthcoming as far as you are concerned," Quimby snapped. "You take even one toothful of booze and I will see to it that you never drink anything again."

"Quimby..."

The Judge didn't answer.

"Quimby..."

"What?"

"Go fuck yourself."

"Now men," Hames interjected swiftly with a greasy smile, oil on troubled waters. "Let's cut this out and get along. We're all in this thing together, and we only hurt ourselves in the end by fighting."

"Bullshit," muttered Dancer, but he was somewhat mollified. "Thing is I *need* a drink," he went on.

Hames studied him. He was shaking a little; his hands were shaking quite a lot.

"Maybe one, Quimby," Hames said. "He's having a rough time."

"One, then."

Hames walked to the desk and Quimby handed him a bottle and glass.

Dancer did indeed need a drink, and he downed it gratefully, closing his eyes on the last drop, sighing wetly, and bowed his head. Quimby wondered if it was in prayer. Hames, seeing the pleasure the man had received, suddenly remembered an appointment he had.

"This afternoon then," Quimby said. "And be prepared for a couple of days, maybe more."

"Don't forget to bring along some support for the man who is giving you the benefit of his superior knowledge," Dancer suddenly said.

Both men were astonished to hear this well-turned phrasing come from the man.

Dancer, seeing their reactions, laughed inside. The bloody damn fools, he was thinking. They knew nothing about him, nothing at all. And by the Lord Harry, they never would.

"We'll meet this afternoon then," Quimby said. "Hames, you and Dancer can ride out together. He's a prisoner on probation in your care. No one has to know your business."

"Where'll we meet you?" Hames asked.

"At the second butte on the way to Tensleep. If I'm not there, wait."

Quimby relighted his cigar, which had gone out. He drew on it, held it in his hand, and examined the ash. Apparently it was satisfactory, for he returned it to his mouth.

"You keep your eye close on him," he said to Hames, nodding his head toward Dancer, without looking at the man.

"Huh!" This word came out of the marshal like a grunt, signifying that he had at least heard.

The buggers, Dancer was thinking as his eyes twisted at them. He had found that his failing vision was better when he squinted. The bastards didn't know a goddamn thing about him. Nobody did, by God, not even Gandy. Gandy didn't know a thing about anything.

His squinting eyes watched the bottle bulging under Hames's jacket. God, he sure could stand a drink!

9

The rooms along the balcony in the Cut-And-Run were small, and they were hot, for with only the one window, which opened onto an alley with the side of another building directly opposite, there wasn't much circulation of air, especially in the summer.

The couple was sleek with sweat, their bodies slithering and slapping as they pounded the squeaking, shaking bed.

"Faster," the girl demanded. "Like that—like that! Oh, my God!"

He was gasping as he drove into her, and as he lifted her legs high and prodded in to the ultimate place she squealed with total delight, while their loins pumped faster and faster and her nails dug into his bucking buttocks. They came in an explosion of maniacal thrashing which almost brought the bed to the floor, and did bring loud comments and laughter from a couple of the other rooms along the balcony.

"My God, Tony girl. You're some, some piece of woman!"

Tony's dark hair was lying all over the pillow. She had been thinking of John Slocum and now she said, "My name is Pony, not Tony." She remembered how he had looked when he'd called her Pony.

"Sorry. I thought you said Tony, not just the first time when we met but every who-knows-how-many-times since," said Clyde Hames, and his thick brow wrinkled in puzzlement.

She snuggled up to him and he instantly melted. "Call me Pony. It's my new name."

"Good enough, Pony."

The marshal of Cracker Creek lay on his back, feeling her leg against his, and wondered how much time he had before he would have to pick up Dancer and head out to the second butte on the trail to Tensleep.

"That's some thing you've got there, Mister Marshal, sir," the girl said as she started to fondle his penis.

Hames felt the blood rushing to his face, and was glad the girl wasn't placed so she could see his face.

"The mare's kicks are caresses to the horse," he said, heavy as always when quoting.

She raised up on an elbow and stared at him in astonishment.

"Well," he said, "since you're a pony, let's see how you can handle this stud horse."

He rolled up onto his knees and reached down and flipped her over onto her stomach, then drew her up by the hips so she was on her hands and knees.

"This is the way the horses do it, Pony." And he drove

his erection into her, mounting her high and hard and all the way from the rear. Reaching under her he grabbed her hanging teats, one in each hand.

His eyes were soft. He had let them be that way so that he could see better. He was watching the distant, snow-capped mountains, not looking at them really, but feeling them with his eyes. Now, closer to where he sat his horse, his eyes met the willows, the long valley below. He was feeling the vista not only with his eyes but with his whole body, the tingling that always reminded him of his boyhood back in Georgia. And he remembered how it was then to be alone with the earth and the sky, and what the redmen called the Four Directions. Yes, as it was now. As he felt it now, in his body, in his skin, in his breath, the breath of everything breathing.

And it must have keened his danger-sense, that instinct where he knew things, an instinct he'd always had since he was a boy, for it told him now that someone had cut his trail. He knew it had to be the band of renegade Shoshone, Long Dog and the dozen or so warriors, and the white girl.

It was no good now to think of Buffalo Horse and how they had spoken together. He was sure the chief knew nothing of this immediate activity with the renegade band. He remembered too that he had not reminded Buffalo Horse of the favor he'd done him those few years back. Still, the chief was not the type to forget. That was obvious in the way the Shoshone had told him to return in three days. But clearly there had been no time for that message to get to Long Dog and his band.

Quickly he pulled his horse off the trail and headed for the creek that he knew must be up ahead by the long, curving line of willows. In moments he was there, walking his pony into the water to lose his trail, but leaving sign that he had headed north, enough to indicate that he had been careless. He knew he was dealing with sharp trackers, and he was hoping they would not be fooled by his "mistake." Then he headed south. A long way down the stream he kicked the horse up the low bank and out of the water at a place where the ground was hard. He rode a few yards, dismounted, then returned to the creek bank to erase any sign he'd left by pulling a loose branch of sage over the ground. At the last moment, as he took a final look around, he saw from the corner of his eye the spotted pony getting ready to urinate. In a flash he had thrown a stone at him and the animal spooked away from his purpose. In the next moment he'd mounted, still holding the branch of sage, and had kicked the horse into a canter. "You can take a leak later, Spotty," he said.

After a couple of hundred yards he lifted the horse to a gallop. He knew they would pick up his trail. But he might have gained some time.

He kept the horse at a good pace, careful not to push him too hard. Fortunately, nightfall was close. He decided that he would pull under cover once the sun was down, and rest for an hour or two. Let the horse blow, rest his legs. Then... then where? Could he circle around and get back to Cracker Creek?

It was chilly in the saloon, Swede Pete and the boy Hendry swept out, arranged the tables and chairs, and threw down a few handfuls of sawdust. It was what they did every morning.

"Build a fire," Swede Pete said, speaking strangely past his toothless gums. "It's cold enough to freeze piss on a coyote's pecker. And shit, it is May time!"

Hendry, the boy who helped him on occasion and ran chores for the Judge and any other important person in town, picked up the axe and, kneeling, began splitting some fresh kindling.

Old Pete watched him for a minute, wanting to be sure he didn't chop off an arm or a leg. He had taken the boy under his care a couple of years back, and they made an interesting pair, sometimes sharing the soddy the old man had just outside town, other times not even speaking to each other, though they shared the chores at the Cut-And-Run.

Soon the room was warm. There were only two customers, left over from the night before, slumped in chairs leaning against the long back wall facing the bar. Above them hung the broken horns of a bighorn sheep. Pete stood looking at the rows of glasses, the bottles of whiskey, rye, and bourbon that ran the length of the big mirror in back of the bar.

Pete didn't mind being a swamper. He liked to keep busy. But he dreamed of returning to his former love, prospecting. He still had his burro, Harriet, who had accompanied him all over the mountains of the region near South Pass, and indeed had been with him when he'd found gold.

It was Swede Pete and Harriet who had found the yellow metal on Coffee Creek and started the rush to the new lode, which resulted in the Golden Pig and Cracker Creek. For two years it had been all boom, even to the point of the railroad planning a spur to fit the spreading town. Passenger service had been planned, not to mention freight, and Cracker Creek had even been surveyed as a likely cattle point for the drives coming up from Texas. The boom drew the attention of the nation's press. It drew prominent people; it drew entrepreneurs, and of course it drew the crooks and the sharpies. The bust came like a sudden clap of thunder one day without even the herald of rain. In the wink of an eye it was all over. The mine flooded, and no one was going to pump it out. Within days the town was a ghost.

All of this had been told and retold verbally, in print, even in song. It was history, folklore, and it was surely apocrypha.

Pete—nobody knew whether he had another name; he himself didn't—rode high with the boom and remained flat as a stomped snake with the bust. The strike hadn't done a damn thing for Pete. Somebody said he bought a new shirt—or maybe it was that he had his old one washed—and that was the only change it made for him. Like any old prospector or self-respecting mountain man, trapper, or cowpoke, Pete loved the action; a child living only in the present, with not even a glance at tomorrow unless it had the rainbow. But he knew how to throw a party, those who'd known him said, he knew how to spend, and nobody would ever forget Lady Sally, his girlfriend and maybe wife. Lady Sally, it had been said, had run the best cathouse in Chicago, and by God here she'd thrown in with Swede Pete. The man undoubtedly had something even more than the golden touch. Sal up and died of the croup, but Pete just kept on moving toward eighty.

Now he was an old man teaching a half-witted young punk how to swamp a saloon and run chores for the asking. Between his burro Harriet and his all-but-dumb sidekick who'd come from nobody knew where, Pete led a life that was anything but lonely.

When John Slocum walked into the Cut-And-Run that particular morning Swede leaned on his broom, squinted at the sheep's head on the wall that had been a good bit shot away with lead, and sucked his gums.

Dutch Hinderman was manning the sober side of the bar that morning and Pete, receiving the nod from the big man with the green eyes and jet-black hair as he strode in, just stood there watching the action. A fly buzzed around his head and lighted on his nose, but Pete didn't move. The fact that he was a host to flies and never bothered them was one of the salient features mentioned by anyone who knew Pete. It was assumed, of course, that he was crazy because he didn't wave them off or slap at them. "The flies like me an' I likes them," he had told people often enough when they asked him about it.

"I'll take a whiskey; bourbon," Slocum said to Dutch Hinderman, who leaned his hard belly against the bar.

Slocum felt the need for a bath. He was trail-dusty, and he was tired, too. It had been a close squeak getting away from the Shoshone. But he'd had a good horse and good luck. He was wondering whether they'd been out to get him especially or whether they were just after any passing traveler. In any case, he would go back to see Buffalo Horse in three days. Meanwhile, he'd see if there was any other way he could go with the girl. He could think of nothing other than a simple raid on the band—alone, probably at night. The risk was tremendous. It would be much better to wait and see whether Buffalo Horse could help him.

When the barman moved away Slocum picked up the bottle and his glass and walked over to a table in the corner of the room, away from the sleeping figures in the two chairs along the back wall.

It wasn't long before Swede Pete, who had been mopping the floor, had moved into his vicinity. Slocum, in fact, had been waiting for him. He knew the swamper never did more than sweep out the place, and he noted that he had already put down some sawdust. So when he started to mop with a damp cloth wrapped around an old broom, Slocum figured he was due for a visitor. It only took a few minutes for the old man to work his way near to where Slocum was sitting.

"I have heerd of you, mister. John Slocum. Yup."

"And I have heard of you, Pete. Part of the history around here, aren't you?"

The old man had not stopped his mopping. "Soon I'll be part of the town bone orchard. Meanwhile, I hear you are looking for something."

"Some—*thing?*" Slocum asked, emphasizing the last part.

"About everybody and his private gunman is also looking for the same." Swede Pete's jaws were working fast on his tobacco; even his shortage of teeth hadn't stopped his appetite or zest for a juicy chew.

Slocum was staring at the man's beard, which was white, pointed, and quivering under the speed of his chewing. His jaws moved so fast it was almost like a nervous twitch. Suddenly he spat a tremendous jet of brown and yellow tobacco and spittle. It hit the spare woodbox in the corner of the room, not far from Slocum's chair.

"You got good aim, Pete."

"Lotta practice, son. You know I gotta burro can do near as good. Harriet can drown a pissant with a shot of tobaccy at ten paces. Well, near enough," he added, lowering one eyelid in a huge wink.

Slocum said, "Like to buy you a drink."

"I'll take what you got there, young feller."

Now, having been formally invited into conversation,

the old boy leaned his improvised mop against the wall—it fell immediately to the floor with a clatter, but he left it—and drew up a chair and sat down with his host.

Suddenly he yawned. "Bin up all night, well just about. Over to the Nugget. You heerd what happened?"

Slocum was about to say he hadn't heard what happened at the Nugget when suddenly J. Orville DeWitt walked into the Cut-And-Run and, seeing him at the table, walked over.

"Slocum, I've been looking for you. Am I interrupting?"

Slocum nodded to a chair, then looked at Swede Pete, who turned halfway toward DeWitt and said, "You got it all writ up in your paper, have ya?"

"About Loming?"

"That was the big news, huh. Just askin' this man here if he knew about it." And without a break to receive an answer he turned to Slocum, saying, "Loming Nosniffer—boy, what a name!—a feller who—"

"The name is Nostrander," DeWitt interrupted.

"I don't give a shit if his name's George Washington. The poor son of a bitch still got his guts spilled last night!" Swede Pete snapped the words out like a barrel full of bullets, his stringy neck quivering with excitement, his creamy old eyes bulging with indignation at DeWitt's interrupting him, and at the same time he very nearly swallowed his chew. But he recovered, racing on with his story. "Slocum here don't know the populace of Cracker Creek and so it don't matter the name. The point is, this feller, who is a famous citizen in this place, got shot up in a game of poker—there was five aces in the game—and look to died when the boys laid him out on a pool table. Somebody called Doc Hogie—"

"Hobie!" snapped DeWitt, and this time he didn't let the old swamper get the story back, but raced on. "Hobie said the man was dying, but not right away. There was blood all over the place. The point was, all this interrupted the poker, the dice, everything. Everybody got taken with it—meaning, was Nostrander going to cash in or not. And when?"

At this point Swede Pete could contain himself no longer.

"Pop Finnegan handled the bets and 'fore you could scratch yer own ass they was bettin' on Hogie or Hobie or whatever the hell his name is that the poor bugger was going to cash in by sunrise—or he wasn't. Next thing you knew the pot was big as a hay wagon!" His words came tumbling out of his mouth, past his chew, his spittle, which he sprayed generously about him, and his whitish gums.

"So what happened?" Slocum asked, making no effort to contain his laughter, though the old sourdough was as serious as a stone. Orville, on the other hand, was relishing every scene of the frantic betting that went back and forth as the patient's condition waxed or waned and the odds plummeted or soared. His nimble mind was already re-creating the entire episode for the readers of the next edition of the *TaleTeller*.

"What happened?" Pete asked. "Why, about a minute before sunrise, Noseniller cashed in his chips."

After their roaring laughter had subsided Slocum turned to Swede Pete. "I understand you do chores and odd jobs around town."

"For a price!"

"Of course." Slocum grinned at the raspy old boy. "I need a good man to help me with something."

"By God, I could tell that the moment I seed you walk

in." Swede Pete whipped off the old peaked cap he was wearing and instantly put it back on his head.

"I'll be going," Orville said, pushing back his chair. Obviously he wished to remain, but Slocum didn't ask him to stay.

When he was gone Slocum said, "I want to hire you, Pete. But it's secret."

"You want me to take you to the mine, the Golden Pig."

Slocum nodded.

"Hell, anybody coulda done that, and you didn't need to roust old Orville outta the place."

"True, except for one thing. I don't want anybody to know it. Nobody. Not even your burro, Harriet."

The old man studied him, sniffing, scratching his shoulder, then the inside of his thigh. He stroked his beard, on which some brown spittle had sprayed.

"I got a feelin' you want somethin' more," he said, and his voice was even more grainy than usual.

"Maybe."

"It'll cost you more."

"That's what I know."

A hot iron running right through his head and neck, down his back. His eyes feeling as though they had been crushed. Pain. God, the pain! He felt vomit rising in his throat and swallowed it. Now it began to come back. The herd, the storm, the taking over Tex Leatherbee's beeves.

Suddenly he felt a stabbing agony in his side as a heavy boot crashed into his ribs.

"Get up!"

"Gandy!"

Again he felt the bile, and this time it slipped past his

tight lips. Then someone grabbed his shoulder and he was switched over onto his back, his head bursting.

He was on the ground, three men standing over him. Now he recognized Leatherbee's voice.

"Weren't quite so smart as you thought, huh, Gandy?" The big Texan's sneer was almost as painful as the agony in his head and body.

Gandy opened his eyes. It came to him that it was a gray sky, and he was glad. Sunlight would not have been so good. It wasn't the first time he'd been conked with a steel barrel, but it was the worst. That big son of a bitch Leatherbee must have done it himself.

The others were approaching now—the kid whose hat and Winchester he'd taken and the other drovers who'd been guarding the herd.

He stood shakily on his feet, his hands together at his waist, looking at them through half-closed eyes. He knew he was bleeding, but he made no move to touch his head or neck. He would not give them the satisfaction.

"Tough old bastard, ain't he, Tex?"

"He was. But he ain't now." Leatherbee was standing very close, so close it hurt his eyes to look at him. "Thought you could pull it off, huh?"

"Near did," Gandy said.

"You never learn, do you, Gandy?"

"I know what I know, Tex."

"Wouldn't fill the asshole on a flea, what you know."

"I know you don't got the guts to stand up to me without your pimps helpin' ya."

The spittle from Tex's big jaws hit him in the face like a bullet. He made no move to wipe it. Instead he spat back right into Leatherbee's face, but missed and hit him in the neck.

SLOCUM AND THE CRACKER CREEK KILLERS 151

The next thing he knew he was on his back, downed by the big Texan's hamlike fist.

"You wanta fight me, I'll fight you," Leatherbee snarled.

Gandy got slowly to his feet.

"Tex, you never did learn to control your temper. That'll get you in trouble one day."

Gandy was at his coolest, and he had always known how to infuriate the big Texan. Though it hurt him badly, he grinned. A big, wide grin.

"You hit me again, Leatherbee, or spit on me, or any of your little boys here try it, you'll never get what you want. You understand me, you big, fat son of a bitch?"

For the young cowhands surrounding the two men, the silence that fell was appalling. No one *ever* talked to Tex Leatherbee like that. No one. Especially an old bugger of forty, maybe more, who'd just been pistol-whipped, kicked, spat on, and generally hammered. They stood waiting in awe, wondering what Big Tex was going to do.

But Tex was silent and Gandy continued.

"Heard you got your ass whipped by that feller Slocum, Leatherbee. Three of you. Fer Christ sake..." And, turning his head slightly, but with his eyes bold on the Texan, he spat at a clump of sage.

A short silence fell on the group, but it was sufficient time for Leatherbee to control himself. He had sense, after all, and he realized that what he was after was bigger than his hatred of Gandy. At least until he got his hands on it. Then... well, that would be another matter.

They stood there, almost nose to nose, neither backing down, yet, strangely it was apparent to all that Gandy had scored. The loser somehow had wiped out the big Texan's victory. And they all knew it. Tex had to swallow it. And Gandy was grinning.

"I'll show you, Leatherbee," he said, speaking carefully, with the minimum of words, to keep the others away from it.

Tex Leatherbee understood. He nodded.

"You keep your boys off me. One funny move and..." He suddenly spread his hands wide apart, palms up, his face bland with innocence. "So kill me. Torture me to death. I can handle twenty, fifty times what you can, Leatherbee. And you know it. So lay off, the bunch of you."

Spitting again aimlessly to show his contempt, Gandy turned and walked over to a rock and sat down. Reaching to his shirt pocket, he took out a quirly and a lucifer.

It was good. It was real good. The quirly. But even better, even better was the way he'd handled Leatherbee and his cowboys.

10

The jays and the chickadees were calling as Slocum rode into the creek that lay at the edge of the Shoshone camp. An eagle sailed high overhead; in his way he was defining the limitless sky. He was well out of sight before he reached the horizon.

Dismounting amidst the stony silence of the camp, Slocum was led by a warrior to the chief's lodge. The three days had passed and Buffalo Horse was expecting him.

"First we will smoke," the chief said. "And then we will talk to the white woman. The chief was wearing a white man's broad-brimmed hat with a single eagle feather sticking up from it.

Three headmen whom Slocum had seen the last time now entered and seated themselves at the fire and accepted the pipe in turn.

When the lodge flap was pulled back to admit someone with a message for the chief Slocum caught a glimpse of

153

the soft movement of goldenrod and blue asters as the wind stirred, blowing the strong horse smell of the pony herd into the lodge.

At last they finished the long pipe and Buffalo Horse said, "We will speak now of the woman, White Painted Flower. Her father wishes to pay a ransom for her, but White Painted Flower is not to sell. But our friend Slow-Come here has asked again; for now the father is older and with his daughter nearer to him now, returned to our country, he is anxious to have her with him." He paused. There was murmuring among the headmen. Slocum said nothing.

The chief resumed. "Long Dog, who has taken White Painted Flower for his wife, does not wish to give her up. Yet he wishes to bring his band back to our village."

He looked directly at Slocum now and said, "We, the headmen of the tribe, have met in council." He paused again and a further murmuring studded the little group.

"I do not wish to tell again to you, a white man, about the white man's injustices to the Shoshone," Buffalo Horse said, "but our young men are restless, and with so many of the white men coming into our country it is more hard to control them. Yet I have always spoken for peace, and so have our tribe's elders. We wish peace now, more than ever. But we wish honor too. Yet you must know that the Indian way is not the white man's way."

"I know that, Buffalo Horse," Slocum said.

"Ho!" said the headmen.

"The council has come to a decision," Buffalo Horse said, "but it is a decision that comes from the people."

"That's fine with me," Slocum said.

"It is that Long Dog will fight the white man for his daughter, with knives."

"But that cannot be," Slocum said. "The father is an old

man, and not well. He is sick. He could not even fight with fists. Never with knives."

At this there was much muttering among the three headmen.

"Ah," Buffalo Horse said. "He is a white man, a Wasichu." His eyes were directly on Slocum now. "This has been thought about, Slow-Come, the white man being old and weak. It is so that Long Dog is young and strong. And so Long Dog can fight the knife fight with Slow-Come."

"Ho!" the headmen said when he had finished. "Ho!"

Slocum understood. It was certainly not the white man's way of thinking, but he saw how they had arrived at the decision that could satisfy all parties. He nodded to the headmen and turned toward Buffalo Horse and said, "Yes."

They had started out with Quimby leading, Dancer in the middle, and Hames bringing up the rear. Dancer, obviously, was not to be trusted, so it was the only sensible arrangement. But they hadn't reckoned on the need for discussion of their plan and Quimby's garrulousness. Hames, of course, could have ridden for a day or two without saying a word. But the Judge was a man who thrived on human intercourse, and felt starved when it was withdrawn. Thus, about halfway through the morning, they rode whenever possible with Dancer a good bit away on their flank; this, of course, not being possible when the trail was narrow. But then they would return to the old format.

Now, reaching a long sweep of flat land with a much wider trail, Quimby quickly ordered their prisoner to move out to their right so that he could converse with Hames. They hadn't discussed their situation for a couple of hours due to the restrictions of the terrain, and Woolf had been feeling peevish. However, the good moment had come, and now he had Hames's ear, with little fear of Dancer overhearing.

"So you're figuring we'll have a clear field," the marshal began, coming right in at the exact point they'd left off two hours earlier.

"Clyde, stop worrying. There will be no one at the place. The only possibility would be Gandy, and as I told you he's being taken care of. In fact, by now he could even be done for."

"But you cannot be sure," Hames said.

"I am sure."

Clyde Hames belched thoughtfully. "He that leaves certainty and trusts to chance,/ When fools pipe he may dance."

"Clyde, I think you make them damn things up yourself."

But the marshal was remorseless this day, following up instantly with a second quotation. "Quit not certainty for hope," he deponed with infuriating righteousness.

The Judge spat angrily over his horse's withers. He was starting to feel quite uncomfortable. First of all, he hadn't ridden in some time, and secondly, he was feeling the twinges of an old case of piles.

His companion had been watching his growing discomfort, but said nothing. The Judge said nothing for fear of having to endure yet another pompous quotation.

But their prisoner, always eager for anything that he might pick up toward helping his survival, had ridden closer to them. Twice he'd been ordered back, earlier that day, but Dancer took pride in a boyhood defiance, and right now he was riding quite close and noting in detail Quimby's problem.

SLOCUM AND THE CRACKER CREEK KILLERS 157

"Looks like you might have a touch of the piles there, Judge," he said cheerily, and his face spread in a wide grin, revealing an opening where two teeth were missing from the upper front of his mouth. This gave him a cheery look at times when he wasn't feeling especially cheerful, and it also enabled him to suck air in with a sort of whistling sound, and to blow it out with the same effect.

"Get back out to the flank there, Dancer." Snarled Quimby, speaking around his pain. "Nobody asked you to listen to our conversation."

Dancer grinned, but he wasn't feeling happy at the Judge's attitude, though his gap in the front row of his teeth belied what he was really feeling. Sometimes people thought he was a fool, with his silly grin and seemingly open manner. But if they acted on this view they generally regretted it. Dancer was almost as tough as his ex-partner, Gandy. It was just that now, in the sunset of his career, he wasn't as fast, as quick-witted, or as remorseless as he was when the Gandy–Dancer gang was terrorizing honest folk all over the country.

The man whom everyone had always known as Dancer, now in his later years, had obviously suffered a great deal in prison. Not being as emotionally tough as his former partner, who had seemed to thrive on the spartan living in the penitentiary, Dancer had aged fast. He'd been written off as finished, just about good enough for the road and that was it. Still, there was one thing that held him together: the loot hidden by Gandy. A good part of it was his, and a lot of it belonged to other members of the gang. He didn't know where Gandy had stashed it, but he had an idea. And he was going to play those two clowns, Quimby and Hames, for every card he could get away with. Hell, anyone who'd been on the owlhoot trail knew that anything could happen. Some men had even been known to get dealt a fifth ace when they needed it. So why not he? Why not?

A little later, Quimby ordered a halt by a creek. He was hurting badly, but he wasn't complaining much. Dancer took note of that. Quimby couldn't be completely bad if he had that much courage. Dancer—about whom nobody knew anything, and he'd taken pains all his life to keep it that way—sure didn't envy the Judge with his piles. He himself had had piles once when he was in the army and had to ride a McClellan saddle. He would never forget that, and he knew the army would never forget him. What he'd done to that son of a bitch Sergeant whatever-his-name-was—he couldn't remember, but he had fixed the bastard good. But that was a long time ago, long before—before he'd gone to medical school, before Janey and . . . and the kid.

"All right, mount up, we're wasting time!" Quimby snapped, feeling better now.

Hames mounted heavily, like a stone man being lifted by some extra power that put him in the saddle. Quimby helped himself by wrapping his fist in his horse's mane for support. Even so, he was awkward; he was awkward even without the piles, Hames thought, watching him.

Dancer was still able to mount easily, though his guts were bad, and his head and eyes. As they rode off, once again in single file with himself in the middle, he was thinking how long ago he had not been "Dancer." That was before a lot of things, for sure. It was before . . . he'd gone to hell.

For a long time the pain was beyond what he could bear. There seemed no area where the fire wasn't burning, the pounding hammers driving him into something small. His breath hurt and he had difficulty seeing. His aim was to sit straight in his saddle and to show nothing. He knew from grim experience that it was easy to get lost in pain. To help him, he remembered his hatred, his purpose. His hatred of Leatherbee and his men, the two who were riding with them now, and his plan to outwit them.

"We are riding one helluva ways," Leatherbee was saying now. "And where the hell are we goin'?"

"Why don't you just ride. We'll get there when we get there," Gandy said.

He was still taking the high hand, not giving an inch, knowing, though, that Leatherbee or one of his two buddies might blow up at him. He wanted them off balance. An angry man, as anyone with any sense knew, was always at a disadvantage in the face of a man who kept his calm. He had to keep calm. Jab at them, push them off-balance so that when they did act they would do so from their irritation, their anger, and not from good sense. It would be he who would have the good sense, always watching, patiently waiting. The prisoner, he had learned in prison, always had a certain advantage over the jailer. If seen in that light, a man did in fact have an advantage. It was how he had managed his escape. He had discovered his jailer's weakness.

"Get yer ass moving, Gandy," one of the cowboys, a young man named Dillman, suddenly shouted from the shadow of some willows where he had stopped up ahead to look back.

Gandy didn't make even the slightest movement. He might not even have heard the man, though he'd bellowed his command.

Suddenly the Texan was galloping back down the trail. Gandy had to exert all his willpower not to react, to remain walking his horse, with his hands tied together in front of him.

As Dillman came pounding up on his tough little cow pony, Tex Leatherbee's voice cut across the trail.

"Dillman, get on up ahead to relieve Barker."

Gandy watched the reluctance in Dillman's face, the near-refusal of the order as he sawed back on his reins and turned his gray pony, almost bringing him up onto his hind legs.

"Gandy, you better straighten up," he snarled in a lower voice so that Leatherbee couldn't hear.

"It'll be a hot day in December when I straighten up for a kid like you, sonny." Gandy grinned—though painfully—as he saw it cut into the drover's face.

But Leatherbee was barking orders down the trail, and it was no moment to cross him. Gandy kept grinning. His timing had been just fine.

An hour later Leatherbee called a halt, holding up his massive right hand as a signal. They were in a clearing with a small creek bordering one side.

"Walk yer horses into the water," the Texan said. "Let 'em freshen their legs, drink a bit. We'll wait here till I see what sense I can get from our scout and guide."

He swung down from his saddle and signaled Gandy to follow suit. It wasn't easy with his hands tied together, but he managed. He would not ask them for anything.

"How far from here, Gandy?" Leatherbee said.

"Not far."

"I ast you a question. You want the boys to work out some of your snot, do you?"

"What do you want, Leatherbee?"

"You know what I want, and you better come up with it. I mean, by Jesus, right now!"

They had walked away from the other two, Dillman and Barker, and Big Tex had lowered his voice so they wouldn't hear. In the meantime, Gandy was figuring a way to play the two men against Leatherbee.

"Be a pity if them two fellers found out what you were up to, Tex. How about that?"

"They won't find out anything from me, and if they do find out something from you then you're a gone goose, Gandy."

Gandy carefully let go a chuckle, for it hurt him to laugh. But he did enjoy the big man's sudden discomfort at the thought of Barker and Dillman wanting to cut in on his business.

"We'll get there soon," Gandy said.

"How soon?"

"Maybe tonight." He paused, chewing a little on his lower lip. "Course, there could be others there ahead of us."

"Others!"

"Sure. You remember Dancer, don't you? I'll bet you and him will be real glad to see each other."

"That son of a bitch'll bleed bourbon when I shoot him, by God, and that's a gut!"

Gandy didn't say anything.

"I am telling you, Gandy, for the last time, don't you try to pull any wool on me, for I'll sure ventilate you, and slowly. I want to get to that cache and then out. You play your part right, I might even give you a little something for your trouble. You cross me, on the other hand, and I will cut your throat. You got me?"

"I sure do." Suddenly he was playing it brisk, as though he'd come to a decision. "We got just a ways to go. Not far. But we want to be careful is the thing."

"Careful? Why careful?"

"On account of there could be Indians about."

"Indians?" Tex Leatherbee's surprise seemed to fill his whole body.

"Used to be about here in the old days."

"But we're at peace with the buggers. They ain't about. Hell, they just ain't *supposed* to be about."

"Dunno, Tex. They used to hang out around here—in those canyons. You could hide a army in there. Nobody'd ever find it."

"Hell, I know that. Shit, didn't we ride in here often enough?" But there was alarm and anger in his voice. "Gandy, you trickin' me? I will carve you to death real slow."

"You know how these canyons are; all like boxes, and rocky as hell. You recollect nobody ever found us in here."

"They sure didn't."

"So what you're lookin' for, chances are good that nobody'd ever find it here either. Am I right?"

"Go ahead. What you gettin' at?"

"That we're here. Now it's been a good long time since I was here, and I got to remember how and where and like all that. We could sure get lost."

"But for Christ sake, the mines are in there. The Golden Pig is in there. What the hell you being so spooky about, damn it? Hell, all kinds of people bin up here in them mines digging and everything else, for Christ's sake! It ain't no mystery, God damn you, Gandy! What the hell you trying to pull!"

"I am not trying to pull anything. The mine is here, that's right. But you don't come in to it this way. It's open on the other side and got a couple of trails up there, even a road, so it's no trouble getting in and out. But on this side

SLOCUM AND THE CRACKER CREEK KILLERS 163

of this bunch of rock canyons it is something else, my friend. And you better handle that. You want in there, you're going to have to handle that!"

"We're close now," Quimby was saying. "I mean, we're close to the Golden Pig. Coming in from another side, that is."

"Sure enough," Dancer said.

"Hell, I could have led the way here. How far now?"

"Not far."

Quimby felt the night falling onto the backs of his hands. The sun was down, and there was a chill in the air.

Dancer felt the evening chill in the wings of his nose. It reminded him of someone he didn't want to think about right now. God, would he ever get it all settled? He wished he had a drink.

"How about a drink, Marshal?"

"How near we be to it now?"

"Close."

"How close, damn it!" snapped Quimby. "*How* close?"

"Yonder."

"At the mine?"

They were at the mouth of a box canyon which was one of a series, a kind of catacomb of canyons, rocky, desolate, yet there had been a time when everyone knew those canyons were loaded with gold.

"Not enough gold in them hills now to fill a tooth, I hear tell," Dancer said. And he spat. "How about that whiskey, Hames?"

"Give it him," Quimby said testily. "Blackmail it is. He'll be so boozed up he'll be leaking bourbon."

Dancer chuckled at that.

"So cut the cackle," Quimby said as Hames poured a

slug of whiskey. And he added, "I'll take some." He waited while Hames poured for the three of them in some tin cups.

"Cut the cackle," Quimby repeated after he'd taken a drink. "And tell me where the place is. How far from here?"

"And in what direction?" Hames added.

"Ain't far," Dancer said, savoring the booze as it flooded his insides, savoring, too, the impatience of his escorts.

"I am asking you where it is," insisted Quimby with an heroic effort to control himself. "Is it a hundred miles from here? A hundred feet? In the mine? Why would Gandy have hidden something in the mine? That would have been real dumb!"

"These canyons look like a good place," Hames said. "Shit, a man could get lost quick as a whistle."

"How close are we?" And there was threat now in Quimby's voice. "You stop playing with us, Dancer!"

"You're that close," Dancer said, "that like if the place had a hand there you could shake."

And he passed his tin cup for seconds.

"The only thing is, I got to try to remember just exactly what one of them box canyons it is. I figure it is that one there, but I ain't for certain sure."

"That one is where the Golden Pig is. Fact, you can see the top of the first shaft." Quimby sniffed.

"Thing is," Hames cut in, "thing is, those canyons—hell, a man can get lost forever in them."

"That's why me and Gandy picked this place for a hideout. Nobody can find you in there. Nobody. And nobody ever did."

"Until that posse caught up with you, Dancer!" said Quimby.

"They didn't catch us here. Nobody ever even *seen* us here."

"That is correct," Clyde Hames said. "But where is the cache?"

"Can't tell till daylight. Better pass that bottle so's I can sleep comfortable and have sweet dreams and wake up in the morning with a clear eye and a steady hand and my memory all ready with it."

Barefoot and stripped to the waist, their bodies were almost identical save for the white man being a bit heavier, broader in the shoulders. Except for a slight paleness of skin, Slocum with his raven-black hair could have been taken for an Indian, too. Long Dog, on the other hand, was less broad in the chest and shoulders, but he was fast. The crowd watching—it was the entire tribe—felt the adversaries were evenly matched.

For a moment they stood facing each other before the signal would be given to start. Each held a buffalo-skinning knife in his hand. Whoever drew first blood would be declared the winner. But there was to be no fight to the finish, no killing, as it would have been in the old days. It was a fight of honor, not to the death.

At a word from Buffalo Horse, the combatants advanced toward each other and began circling.

The village had gathered in a meadow not far from where they were camped, forming a circle around the two fighters. It was a hot day. The sun bore down on their bare backs. However, neither felt it. Each one's concentration was on the other.

Suddenly Long Dog charged, his knife blade almost

blinding in the brilliant sun. Slocum fell back, sidestepping and slashing with his knife.

Now Slocum followed the Shoshone warily, sweeping his sharp blade from left to right. A murmur rose as the point of Slocum's blade cut one of the Indian's leggings.

All at once Long Dog sprang forward and now there was a loud murmur from the spectators as his blade whistled through the white man's hair, but drew no blood. Fortunately, Slocum had been moving away as the Shoshone struck.

Now Long Dog darted in and instantly sprang away; again he feinted, ducked, bobbed and weaved, with Slocum circling so that he was always facing his man.

Long Dog sprang forward and this time Slocum didn't spring away but threw up his arm so that both their knife arms locked in mid-air. At the same moment Slocum's free arm circled the Shoshone's neck, while Long Dog grabbed Slocum around the waist in a bear hug.

Locked together, they went into a kind of dance as each tried to trip the other. Slocum suddenly kicked Long Dog's ankle and brought him to the ground. Locked together, neither let go his grip as they rolled in the grass.

Suddenly Long Dog stabbed his thumb into Slocum's eye and when the white man's hold slipped he broke free. Then, rolling swiftly across the clearing, he was up on his feet. Yet Slocum was equally fast and now stood facing him.

Suddenly the Indian charged, and Slocum stuck out his leg. As the Indian went down he nicked him on the side of his shoulder with the point of his skinning knife.

But before Buffalo Horse could step forward to touch the winner, a runner had burst through the crowd and stood before the chief. A loud murmur had started through the crowd. It took Slocum a moment to realize what had happened.

Chief Buffalo Horse held up his arms.

"The pony soldiers are coming," he said in a strong voice which carried to the farthest edges of the crowd. "They are at Owl Creek. They will be here before the sun touches the tops of the pine trees."

Long Dog meanwhile was calling his band together.

"They have come for Long Dog," somebody shouted.

Within minutes Long Dog and his people were on their horses and riding fast out of camp. As they sped away, Slocum caught a glimpse of the white girl, Felicia. White Painted Flower.

He didn't hesitate. In a matter of moments he had saddled and bridled a sleek buckskin pony someone had brought him from Buffalo Horse, and was pounding after the fleeing Long Dog's band.

11

The sun hammered down in silence onto the tops of the rimrocks, its light burning into the box canyons, the rocks, ledges, crevices, and caves of the jagged terrain to the north of the Golden Pig mine and the other empty shafts that were still flooded with water.

"Isn't there anyone at the Golden Pig?" Dancer had asked, wiping his sweating forehead.

"Nobody supposed to be," Hames replied brusquely. Both he and Quimby were starting to wonder about their man's inability to remember the way to the cache. Halfway to noon they were more worried as Dancer had led them up and down and back and forth looking, as he put it, for an old game trail.

"He put it in one of them caves," Dancer said. "But I didn't actually see him doin' it."

Quimby grabbed him by the collar, his face livid. "What the hell d'you mean—you didn't actually see him stashing the money? You said you *knew* where it was hid! You son of a bitch, I got a notion to break your neck in pieces, Dancer!"

It was at that moment of crescendo that a calm voice suddenly cut into the scene.

"Why lookey here; lookey here! By jingo, if it ain't the marshal of Cracker Creek himself in person, and the good Judge in person, and Mr. Dancer, the famous Western outlaw!"

The soft Texas drawl fell on them like the clap of disaster, which it was. They turned to see themselves confronted by Tex Leatherbee, his two cowboys, and Clay Gandy.

"My God, you caught him, Leatherbee. Congratulations, man!" roared Quimby with badly feigned delight. It was an heroic failure at trying to carry off the disastrous turn of events that had brought them down.

But Quimby would not give up easily. He glared at Hames to pull himself together and started toward Tex with his hands outstretched in greeting. "Tex, you old devil! I knew you'd catch him. I just knew it! There's a bonus in it for you."

"You got Gandy, then," Hames said, slow as molasses to pick up on the speed of Quimby's response to the situation.

Tex was dangerously silent, a grim smile playing in his eyes and at the corners of his lips. Now, as Quimby approached, he stepped aside nimbly and tripped him. The Judge crashed to his knees on the iron-hard ground, crying out with pain.

"Sorry there, Judge. But I ain't your buddy. I would like to know what you three clowns are doing up here." He glared at Dancer. "You showin' them the sights, Dancer? You double-crossin' son of a bitch!" He stepped forward, swift as a man half his size, and slammed his fist right into Dancer's thin, bony chest. The blow knocked Dancer flat on his back, where he remained, moving slightly under the great pain he was experiencing, but not crying out.

"Leatherbee, whyn't you hit somebody least half your size, you big fat son of a bitch!" It was Gandy. Gandy standing steady as a whip, unarmed, cut though no longer bleeding, with welts and bruises all over his body. But standing there.

"Shut up!" Leatherbee said. "By God, there are just too damn many people in on this here party. I think some of you need buryin'."

"Don't be a damn fool," Gandy said. "That there is the Judge of Cracker Creek and that is the town marshal, as you well know. You kill them, the law will chase you to China and back. God, why are you so damn dumb!"

He was chuckling to himself as he spoke, moving about a little—not too much, not too close to Dillman and Barker, nor to Leatherbee either.

"Come off it, Gandy," snarled Leatherbee. "This is it. This is the end of the trail. Where's the cache?"

A chuckle started in Gandy's throat and suddenly burst out of him in a loud laugh. "You stupid clowns! You think I'd show you where there was a cache, even if there was one?"

"I could put a bullet right into your guts!" Tex had drawn his big Navy Colt and drawn back the hammer.

"Slow down. I never told you there was a cache."

"The hell you didn't!"

Gandy was shaking his head. "Nope. It was *you* told *me*. I never told you a damn thing. Think about that, you damn fool!"

"But you told us!" Quimby suddenly wheeled on Dancer. "You said you knew where it was. Dancer!"

"No, I said I thought I might maybe know something about where to try to locate it. I never said I *knew!*"

"Jesus Christ," Gandy said with mock despair. "What can a man do with such goddamn fools in this world?"

He had been moving around as he talked, but now suddenly stopped, obviously listening. "Hold it!" He held up his hand, palm out, to silence them. "We got company," he said. "And I don't think they're bringing any cake for tea."

One of the cowboys suddenly screamed, "Red Bastards!"

A shot rang out.

"What the hell . . . ?" Dancer started to say when suddenly an arrow hit his chest and ran all the way through him. The impact drove him backward where he fell flat on the ground, and now they all saw the Shoshone racing up toward them from all sides.

Slocum had ridden hard after Long Dog and his band. He knew the Indian wouldn't be expecting anyone to follow him; he and his band were intent only on getting away from the soldiers. But Slocum was pretty sure that the army was there only in an investigating capacity. They might not know that Long Dog and his band were at hand, though they were very likely looking into the depredations that the renegades had wreaked upon some of the sodbusters along the Greybull valley. They would be dropping in on Buffalo Horse for a powwow.

Certainly from Long Dog's view it made the best sense to cut and run. But Slocum had seen the girl riding off with them. It didn't look as though Long Dog had seriously considered rejoining Buffalo Horse's lodge; it looked more like he was trying to hole up until things cooled down for him and his band.

Clearly the chief had seen through that; indeed, he had accused Long Dog of lying. But why had he proposed the knife fight? Was it maybe to show up Long Dog before his own people, maybe even before himself? Slocum had long known that Buffalo Horse was one of the shrewdest of the Indian chiefs.

Well, the chief had taken a gamble on him, he realized; and on himself probably as well. He was that kind. Perhaps now he hoped that Long Dog would see what a damn fool he was and would buckle down. But first it had been necessary to bring Long Dog down to earth. Maybe the knife fight, with Slocum defeating him, had accomplished the trick.

The Indians were riding fast. Slocum kept well back on their trail, knowing they would surely keep a sharp lookout. He had to be careful. Long Dog had not been a graceful loser, he had seen in that brief moment after the fight, before the crier came in announcing the arrival of the army.

He was wondering if the band had a special destination or were just trying to put distance between themselves and the soldiers. Rounding a low cutbank he pulled up fast on his reins, bringing the buckskin to a hard stop. Long Dog had stopped his band in a small clearing near a creek. They were preparing to rest and water their horses. Slocum realized they must have dropped a scout on their back trail to see if they were being followed. Probably the man would be closer to the band, but he had to be extra careful now.

Dismounting, he led the buckskin into a thick clump of cottonwoods, then took out his field glasses and, finding a good place to watch without being seen, he trained the glasses right onto the Indians. Right off he recognized

Long Dog and a couple of others. And then he saw the girl. She was seated away from the others, quietly by herself.

Cautiously he looked about to see where their rear guard might be. Then he spotted him, down the trail to the right of the small area where the Indians were collected. He felt relief running through him at the realization that he hadn't been spotted.

In only a short while the group below began to stir and mount up, and in another few moments they were again on their way. Slocum was immediately up on the buckskin and, with his eye on their rear guard, began to follow. When he saw the guard rejoin the main body of warriors, he moved in closer.

In another hour they had reached the big honeycomb of box canyons and rock formations and caves that formed the escarpment which had been described to him as the south side of the Golden Pig mining operation. In fact, with the glasses trained on the rocks, he could now detect what he figured must be the side of a cabin.

He understood the mine was still deserted, still not in operation, though it was expected to start up soon. His eyes swept the high desolate area of rock, shrub, tamarack, pine, and spruce. A tough place to get into, he could see, and likely just as tough to get out of.

While the Shoshone up ahead were listening to something Long Dog was telling them, Slocum took the moment to check his weapons again: the Sharps in its saddle holster, his handgun holstered at his side, his derringer holdout inside his shirt, and especially the Arkansas throwing knife strapped to his leg.

The Shoshone had dismounted and were leading their horses up a long, steep incline that rose to the base of the high rocks. He supposed they knew of a way in. There must be dozens of hiding trails in such a place, he thought. But they wouldn't be heading for the mine. They must know of a place where they could hide, and where they would be well protected.

The leaders of the band were quite close to the base of the nearest rock wall when suddenly Slocum, still looking through the glasses, saw something flash and knew in the next moment it had to be gun metal as the shot rang out. He saw one of the Indians topple. In the next instant he saw two near-naked figures high up on the rocks above the place where the shot had come from. When they stood up he saw the bows and arrows, watched the arrows fly toward their chosen targets, and wondered if anyone had been hit.

But this was no time, he felt, to be a spectator. They could be miners up there, or maybe surveyors. In any case, they had fired on Long Dog's band and were now reaping the reward. Even so, it was up to him to help them.

Slocum had spotted what looked like another trail leading up to the big walls of rock, but far to the side of where the pitched battle had started. As he galloped at top speed to his objective he hoped that Long Dog's people were all too busy to see him.

Fortunately there was good cover and he took full advantage of it, soon making it to the ledge he had spotted through the glasses, in good time to train his Sharps on a cluster of Long Dog's warriors.

The boom of the mighty Sharps clearly surprised them, and might even have reminded some of the fighting with the soldier. In any event, Slocum pulled the same trick as he had before, firing, then moving his position, shouting orders in different voices as he did so, giving the impression of several men attacking.

He shot two of the Indians, and saw that someone from the rocks above got another. Now the warriors began to retreat, mounting their horses and riding swiftly back down the long incline. Slocum figured they were thinking of the chance that the army might hear the shooting. In any case, they were playing it close, not being reckless at all. Whatever the reason, it was a lucky moment for the men in the rocks above, whoever they were.

As he dismounted and began to lead his horse farther up toward the high rocks behind the mine shafts, Slocum knew that if he was going to get hold of Quimby's daughter it was going to have to be pretty soon. He knew Long Dog wasn't going to stick by his agreement. It was more than obvious, he realized as he saw the yellow-haired woman riding away fast on the little spotted pony, surrounded by Shoshone warriors.

The first person he recognized when he arrived at the top of the escarpment was Gandy, but the first voice he heard was Tex Leatherbee's. And Leatherbee was holding a big Navy Colt.

"Well, lookey here—another treasure hunter, by God."

"Maybe the man's looking for you, Tex," Gandy said.

"Shut up," the big Texan said, his words falling into a silence. Slocum had said nothing since his arrival.

Hames had been nicked in the arm, though not his gun arm; Quimby hadn't suffered a scratch, nor had Leatherbee. But Dillman and Barker had been creased. No one had been seriously hurt save Dancer, who was dead. Gandy was still suffering from the beating he'd received from Tex and his two cohorts.

"You came just in time for the party," Tex said now. He

moved the gun barrel slightly as a gesture of inclusion which Slocum understood.

"Nice running into you again, Tex."

"Won't have no hoss to help you this time, Slocum."

Gandy was chuckling. "You looking for something up here, mister? All these birds are."

"I just saved your asses with my Sharps. Leatherbee, you keep that gun off me. Do you hear what I am saying!"

"If you got no business up here, Slocum, then ride on."

"Be easy to jump him, Slocum," Gandy said. "I mean, the two of us."

"You'll get a gut full of lead," Leatherbee said, and he nodded toward Dillman and Barker.

Gandy grinned.

"Are you staying out of it, Slocum?" Leatherbee's eyes were hard on him.

"I am not interested in what you all appear to be looking for." His eyes dropped onto Quimby and Hames, both of whom looked away.

"Good enough." Tex turned to his two helpers. "We'll start with Gandy, then."

"You got something you want to ask me?" Gandy said.

"I am not asking any more. I want to know where that cache is, and right now!"

"You're almost standing on it," Gandy said, and he laughed as he watched the shock hit them all.

"Tell it, you son of a bitch!" Leatherbee was getting more and more angry. Slocum's arrival had clearly thrown him, for he hadn't counted on having to deal with someone not concerned with the loot. Yet he did have an old score to even.

"That rock there, that long slab," Gandy said, nodding

to a big rock lying flat on the ground only a few feet from where they were all standing.

Leatherbee threw his eyes at Dillman and Barker. "Move it," he said.

Slocum was watching the proceedings closely, but he was also fully aware of Gandy, noting the great change that had taken place in him since he'd seen him on his arrival in the Cut-And-Run not at all long ago.

"Could be heavy," Gandy was saying. "It's been there a good while of years. Better get some men on it, not those kids."

Dillman and Barker both flushed at that, but Leatherbee snapped at them to get a move on.

"My God," murmured Quimby in awe. "You mean to tell us that cache, that horde has been there right underfoot all these years. Nobody even suspected!"

Gandy chuckled.

Hames drew himself up and said, "Of lawful wealth the devil takes the half; of unlawful the whole and the owner too."

"Jesus," said Tex Leatherbee.

"With all due respect," Hames said in his most wooden voice, "the quotation is actually from Juvenal."

"By God, that is just what I thought," Gandy said with a rolling laugh.

Slocum saw that the man wasn't missing a thing. He was for sure up to something.

Barker and Dillman had managed finally to move the rock. Slocum noted it wasn't as heavy as they were making out. Clearly, they were getting tired of Leatherbee's ordering them the way he did, and also they didn't care a great deal for manual labor.

SLOCUM AND THE CRACKER CREEK KILLERS 179

With the rock moved away to expose a hole, the gathering moved forward for a better look.

"Stand back," said Leatherbee, with his gun still on the others, all of whom were disarmed except for Slocum. He took a look into the hole.

Reaching down with his left hand he lifted out a gunbelt, a holster, and a Deane & Adams sixgun partially wrapped in a cloth, evidently to prevent damage through dirt or rust.

"That's my old hogleg," Gandy said. "I put it in there for good luck. All the best road agents do that, you know. I mean, they do that in Australia. Don't know about here." He sniffed as he watched Leatherbee handling it. "It's not loaded," he said. "Like I said, it was put there just for custom."

"Against the evil spirits," said Clyde Hames.

"Quite!" Gandy smiled agreeably at this understanding of the marshal's.

"Lift the box out," Leatherbee said, waving his gun at his two cowboys. It was obvious to everyone now that they too were under the gun, that, of course, Big Tex was going to take it all.

Slocum watched the sweat stand out on the Texan's big forehead. And he noticed from the corner of his eye that Gandy had edged closer to his captor.

The men had raised a fairly large steel box with a padlock that wasn't something anyone could open on the spur of the moment.

"You got a key?" Tex said, his big eyes bugging at Gandy.

"Search me—no! But you can shoot the lock off, Tex."

"I know that." He had turned his gun toward the box, but then he stopped and picked up the Deane & Adams.

"Might be good to use this one, if it's loaded, and I am sure it is," he said.

"It isn't loaded," Gandy said. "Anyway, ammo would be useless by now, even with the cloth which we saw had fallen away from the gun. But try it if you wish. We've got all day."

Later, Slocum realized the bandit had chosen exactly the right thing to say. Leatherbee lifted the gun and pulled the trigger once, twice, three times on an empty chamber, then threw the gun down.

He lifted his own gun now and shot the lock off. At a sign his two men stepped forward and opened the lid.

There was no stopping everyone from moving forward for a look now, even if Tex had a goosegun trained on them.

It was immediately evident why the box had been so heavy. It was weighted with rocks. Otherwise there was nothing in it.

"You son of a bitch!" screamed Tex Leatherbee.

"Somebody got here first," Gandy said, spreading his hands apart to emphasize his innocence. "I'm not surprised. You clowns with your big mouths let everybody know there was a cache, so somebody found it. Hell! *I'm* the one who ought to be angry, not you. All that work I put into those years!"

"Damn! Damn!" Quimby was cursing now. "Damn it to hell! All these years and to find—rocks! Hell!"

"But you have your mines, Quimby," Slocum said.

"Yes, the town has the mine, Slocum. The Golden Pig."

"And you have the others," said Hames, speaking up, with anger in his voice. "Remember, Quimby: 'Opportunity makes the thief'!"

SLOCUM AND THE CRACKER CREEK KILLERS 181

"Hames, shut your mouth. You don't know what you're talking about."

"I know you've been out here with those men who're going to pump the water. And I know you're planning to pump not just the Golden Pig, not just Number Three Shaft, but the others as well, but with your signature on the deeds."

"You son of a bitch!"

"That'll be enough," Leatherbee said, holstering his sixgun. He turned to Dillman and Barker. "We'll keep Gandy just to make sure he's telling the truth. The rest of you can beat it." He threw his eyes suddenly at Slocum. "Exceptin', I'll be catching up with you, mister. I've got a score to settle with you." Leatherbee's voice changed as he said, "Better cover up that hole." And he nodded to his cowboys.

It was in that very next instant that Gandy stepped forward and snatched up the Deane & Adams that was out of its holster and lying where Leatherbee had tossed it.

One of the cowboys yelled, but afterwards nobody remembered it. Gandy had lifted the gun and had shot Big Tex Leatherbee right in the middle of his guts.

With an awful surprise on his face, the big man sank to the ground, while Gandy held the gun on his two cowboys.

"There are two more in here, boys. Just make the right move and you can have them."

Leatherbee was on the ground, his voice gargling as he tried to speak. "I—I didn't know it was loaded."

"That's what the last dead man said." Gandy was smiling.

"You said it wasn't . . ."

"Don't you know you should never trust a liar?" Gandy said.

182   JAKE LOGAN

Quimby, Hames, and the two cowboys were standing awestruck at the rapid change of scene Gandy had engineered.

"Jesus," Hames said. His use of the deity's name in vain caused Quimby to stare at him.

"I'll be riding out," Gandy said, bending down to take Tex's gun, then moving over to the pile of stacked weapons belonging to the others. With his free hand he threw some of them high into the far rocks, but he kept two, which he shoved into his belt.

"And yours, Slocum."

Slocum unbuckled and handed his gunbelt to the grinning Gandy.

"Sorry, Slocum, but you'll all have your horses. Fact, I'll also be taking your Sharps. In a minute," he said quickly.

Slocum was thinking of the holdout he carried inside his shirt, and he wondered if Gandy was too. To make sure he would, he moved his hand slightly and twisted his shoulder a little as though freeing something inside his shirt. He had kept the move hardly noticeable, not wanting to overplay his hand.

"And that holdout," Gandy said, his grin spreading.

"I think I hear visitors," Slocum said suddenly.

"Cut the shit, Slocum. Give me that holdout."

Slocum reached into his shirt, saying, "I'm not surprised the Shoshone came back. It's what I've been thinking they might do. Can't you hear that?"

"Bring that gun out easy."

"Take good care of it; she's a good one," Slocum said as he placed the derringer carefully on a nearby rock, half crouching as he did so. Gandy was grinning again.

He was still grinning when Slocum rose, drawing the

SLOCUM AND THE CRACKER CREEK KILLERS 183

Arkansas throwing knife from its leg scabbard and watching it sink right into Gandy's chest. He was dead as he hit the ground, and Slocum had grabbed his gun and had everyone covered.

Slocum hadn't been fooling about hearing the Indians. He had thought that Long Dog was maneuvering when he withdrew from the firefight on the south side of the escarpment. But now the Shoshone had circled around and were attacking from the north, through the mining area.

Unfortunately there was a shortage of guns amongst Hames, Quimby, and the two Texans. But Slocum had his weapons and he handed his derringer over to Quimby, and Gandy's Deane & Adams to Hames. It was obvious to them all now that Gandy had visited the spot before he'd come to Cracker Creek, and had taken the loot and hidden it somewhere.

Right now there was no time for thoughts of loot. The Indian attack was brisk. Long Dog was pushing for a quick victory and, Slocum presumed, revenge on himself for the humiliation of the knife fight.

Still, it was the Sharps that proved the equalizer, and by nightfall the Indians had not breached the defenses of the men at the top of the escarpment.

"We'll not get through the night," Hames told Slocum. "And we're low on ammunition. What can we do?"

"We can attack them," Slocum said. "But let me try something first."

Quickly he got the men together and outlined his plan.

"It sounds to me like they're getting low on ammo too. I think their attack is mostly being pushed by Long Dog's anger. It's getting to be dark now, and I figure they're going to try to overrun us."

184   JAKE LOGAN

They had just got settled into the places he had assigned them when the Shoshone attacked. It was the moment when the burning sun was right at the horizon, burning into their eyes as they faced the attackers. It was what Slocum had figured on, now as he slipped down and around a pile of rocks and worked his way to the edge of the Indian attack. Looking down the long descent from the front of the mine, he thought he knew where the girl would be.

In a few moments, as the Indians charged the rocks above, he had hurried down to the little group at the bottom, which consisted of two warriors and the girl. The rest of the band were busy with Long Dog, attacking the hastily thrown up fort above.

The surprise on the faces of the two warrior guards was final as Slocum kicked one in the crotch and slammed his fist into the other's neck. Both blows were ultimate.

"Come on," he said, grabbing the girl's hand.

But she pulled away. "No."

By now he'd had enough and swift as a whistle he had whipped out the throwing knife and had it pointed right under her chin. "You're coming with me—or else," he said, and he wasn't fooling. Indeed, he was wondering whether to knock her out with a punch to the jaw or the temple.

In a moment he had pulled her, half dragged her back up to the little group at the top of the rocks. Hames, left with the Sharps, had accounted for three of the attackers, who were now thinking twice about pursuing Long Dog's aim.

Suddenly Slocum saw the young Shoshone charging toward him from only a few feet away. He only just had time to let go of the girl and duck the whistling tomahawk that would have cut his head in two if it had hit.

In the next moment he had received the full impact of Long Dog's charge, fallen purposely, rolled onto his back, and kicked up into his attacker's groin with his hard boot. The Indian went flying. And when Slocum got to his feet Long Dog was lying on his back, out cold.

It was enough to break the attack. The Shoshone melted away.

The damage wasn't major. One of the Texas cowboys had been wounded—Dillman—though not badly. They decided to wait until morning before heading back to Cracker Creek. Slocum had insisted on it, in fact, for he didn't trust Long Dog not to try another attack, especially now that he had lost the girl.

The mining shack was big enough for Woolf Quimby and Felicia to spend some hours together. Quimby broke down and cried when he saw his girl. In a moment, she was crying too. Slocum left them alone. He had the sudden feeling that the girl didn't want to leave Long Dog and his band.

In the early morning he found her seated on a rock outside the cabin, looking down toward the long stretch of land that ran toward Cracker Creek. He wondered if she'd been there all night. Quimby was alone in the cabin. Slocum could hear him snoring.

"You want to go back?" he asked as she moved so he could sit down beside her.

She shrugged. "I don't know."

He looked at her. She was beautiful.

"Three years, was it? That's a good piece of time to be somewhere where maybe it means something, and then you've got to leave."

She nodded. Turning his head, he could see the tears on

her cheeks. "It—it was very hard," she said. "Hard. Oh, God, at times I wanted to die."

"But..."

"And at times it was... wonderful."

"And in between it was the way it was."

"You're an understanding man, Mr. Slocum."

"I try to be. How is your father?"

"Dad's like he's always been. He hasn't changed."

"Don't you want to see your mother, your brothers and sisters?"

She looked rueful then. "All fourteen of them?" She shook her head. "I don't think so. See, I don't know if Dad told you. They're not my brothers and sisters. He adopted them all. *I'm* his daughter. At least that's what he's told me, and I guess I believe him."

"And your mother?"

"She's his second wife. My mother ran off with a cowboy, Dad said."

"And you...?"

"I guess I ran off with a Shoshone."

They were silent for a long moment.

Then Slocum said, "I'd like to get to know you, Felicia. I like your looks, the way you handle yourself."

"Yeah... I know."

She had turned her head and was looking at him in a way he liked. A soft way, a way that seemed surely to see him. It was not a usual kind of look.

"I heard an Indian once—he was an old man—and he said that being Indian wasn't so much a matter of blood, but a way of being. You know what I mean?"

She shook her head. "I just want to be quiet for a while."

"That's what I know," Slocum said. "Maybe that's what I'm saying."

When Quimby came out of the cabin after a while and said good morning, she was smiling.

JAKE LOGAN

___ 0-425-09088-4	THE BLACKMAIL EXPRESS	$2.50
___ 0-425-09111-2	SLOCUM AND THE SILVER RANCH FIGHT	$2.50
___ 0-425-09299-2	SLOCUM AND THE LONG WAGON TRAIN	$2.50
___ 0-425-09212-7	SLOCUM AND THE DEADLY FEUD	$2.50
___ 0-425-09342-5	RAWHIDE JUSTICE	$2.50
___ 0-425-09395-6	SLOCUM AND THE INDIAN GHOST	$2.50
___ 0-425-09479-0	SEVEN GRAVES TO LAREDO	$2.50
___ 0-425-09567-3	SLOCUM AND THE ARIZONA COWBOYS	$2.75
___ 0-425-09647-5	SIXGUN CEMETERY	$2.75
___ 0-425-09896-6	HELL'S FURY	$2.75
___ 0-425-10016-2	HIGH, WIDE AND DEADLY	$2.75
___ 0-425-09783-8	SLOCUM AND THE WILD STALLION CHASE	$2.75
___ 0-425-10116-9	SLOCUM AND THE LAREDO SHOWDOWN	$2.75
___ 0-425-10188-6	SLOCUM AND THE CLAIM JUMPERS	$2.75
___ 0-425-10419-2	SLOCUM AND THE CHEROKEE MANHUNT	$2.75
___ 0-425-10347-1	SIXGUNS AT SILVERADO	$2.75
___ 0-425-10489-3	SLOCUM AND THE EL PASO BLOOD FUED	$2.75
___ 0-425-10555-5	SLOCUM AND THE BLOOD RAGE	$2.75
___ 0-425-10635-7	SLOCUM AND THE CRACKER CREEK KILLERS	$2.75
___ 0-425-10701-9	SLOCUM AND THE RED RIVER RENEGADES (on sale March '88)	$2.75
___ 0-425-10758-2	SLOCUM AND THE GUNFIGHTER'S GREED (on sale April '88)	$2.75

Please send the titles I've checked above. Mail orders to:

BERKLEY PUBLISHING GROUP
390 Murray Hill Pkwy., Dept. B
East Rutherford, NJ 07073

NAME_____

ADDRESS_____

CITY_____

STATE_____ZIP_____

Please allow 6 weeks for delivery.
Prices are subject to change without notice.

POSTAGE & HANDLING:
$1.00 for one book, $.25 for each additional. Do not exceed $3.50.

BOOK TOTAL	$_____
SHIPPING & HANDLING	$_____
APPLICABLE SALES TAX (CA, NJ, NY, PA)	$_____
TOTAL AMOUNT DUE PAYABLE IN US FUNDS. (No cash orders accepted.)	$_____